"I intend to make love to you."

Beth swallowed, but she didn't back away. Omar wrapped his arms around her and pulled her into an embrace. When his lips found hers, she responded without hesitation.

It took only seconds for the kiss to flame through his blood.

Omar knew he was making a mistake. Beth Bradshaw was the woman he would have to betray before the month was out. To protect his people and his heritage, he would have to deceive her. She would be labeled a failure, even though her theories were one hundred percent right. And he would be the tool of her destruction.

Yet, he couldn't resist her.

D0974819

Dear Harlequin Intrigue Reader,

We've got another month of sinister summer sizzlers lined up for you starting with the one and only Familiar—your favorite crime-solving black cat! Travel with the feisty feline on a magic carpet to the enchanting land of sheiks in Caroline Burnes's *Familiar Mirage*, the first part of FEAR FAMILIAR: DESERT MYSTERIES. You can look for the companion book, *Familiar Oasis*, next month.

Then it's back to the heart of the U.S.A. for another outstanding CONFIDENTIAL installment. This time, the sexiest undercover operatives around take on Chicago in this bestselling continuity series. Cassie Miles launches the whole shebang with *Not on His Watch*.

Debra Webb continues her COLBY AGENCY series with one more high-action, heart-pounding romantic suspense story in *Physical Evidence*. What these Colby agents won't do to solve a case—they'll even become prime suspects to take care of business…and fall in love.

Finally, esteemed Harlequin Intrigue author Leona Karr brings you a classic mystery about a woman who washes up on the shore sans memory. Good thing she's saved by a man determined to find her *Lost Identity*.

A great lineup to be sure. So make sure you pick up all four titles for the full Harlequin Intrigue reading experience.

Sincerely,

Denise O'Sullivan
Associate Senior Editor
Harlequin Intrigue

FAMILIAR
MIRAGE
CAROLINE
BURNES

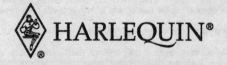

HARLEQUIN®

TORONTO • NEW YORK • LONDON
AMSTERDAM • PARIS • SYDNEY • HAMBURG
STOCKHOLM • ATHENS • TOKYO • MILAN • MADRID
PRAGUE • WARSAW • BUDAPEST • AUCKLAND

ISBN 0-373-22669-1

FAMILIAR MIRAGE

Copyright © 2002 by Carolyn Haines

Visit us at www.eHarlequin.com

Printed in U.S.A.

ABOUT THE AUTHOR

Caroline Burnes continues her life as doorman and can opener for her six cats and three dogs. E. A. Poe, the prototype cat for Familiar, rules as king of the ranch, followed by his lieutenants, Miss Vesta, Gumbo, Chester, Maggie the Cat and Ash. The dogs, though a more lowly life form, are tolerated as foot soldiers by the cats. They are Sweetie Pie, Maybelline and Corky.

Books by Caroline Burnes

HARLEQUIN INTRIGUE

Don't miss any of our special offers. Write to us at the following address for information on our newest releases.

Harlequin Reader Service
U.S.: 3010 Walden Ave., P.O. Box 1325, Buffalo, NY 14269
Canadian: P.O. Box 609, Fort Erie, Ont. L2A 5X3

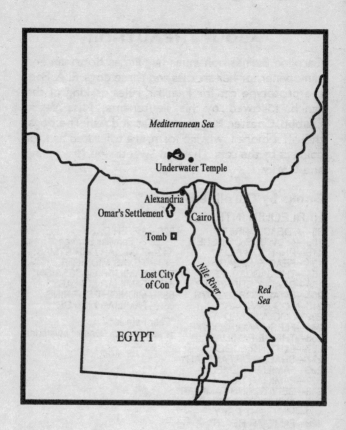

CAST OF CHARACTERS

Familiar—While traveling in Egypt with Eleanor and Peter, Familiar (viewed as a god by the Egyptians) becomes involved with a beautiful U.S. anthropologist.

Beth Bradshaw—Finding the lost City of Con is Beth's mission, and the act that could cement her career. The vast Egyptian desert is dangerous, but not nearly as dangerous as the guide she hires to lead her expedition.

Omar Dukhan—Desert born and European educated, Omar is a man caught between a rock and a hard place. He must choose between duty and love—before Beth is killed.

Harad Dukhan—Harad has forsaken his heritage, but has he also given up his honor and brother?

Bettina Nazar—He's the man with the money and the impetus behind Beth's quest for the lost city. A man who prefers the shadows to the light, he has endless funds and a strong desire to remain faceless and nameless.

John Gilmore—Jealous, petty and a whiner, John makes the trip aggravating for Beth, but he is also an expert at his job. When several other scientists mutiny, John stands by Beth, but is it all a farce?

Mauve Killigan—Not only is Mauve a scientist, she's Beth's friend. In the dangerous and competitive race to find the lost city and the treasures it may hold, Mauve stands to lose a lot—including her life.

Amelia Corbet—Beth's adopted sister lives in New York and works for one of the top public-relations firms in the nation. When Beth calls for help, will be she able to answer?

To Dianna—
A good friend and animal lover.
Many thanks for your friendship.

Chapter One

The world is a strange and wondrous place! Alexandria, Egypt! Imagine. I stepped off that big jet plane and into a world where humanoids have finally come to their senses—they're all cat worshipers.

My fellow felines are all around me, lounging in the airport as if they owned the place. Of course, cats are so far advanced in thought and spirit that we understand that "owning" anything is ridiculous. But it is refreshing to see a culture where humans know their place.

Ah, Egypt. Home of the Sphinx, Cleopatra, the Sahara Desert and a million and one magical dreams. Peter, my humanoid and veterinarian, is here to discuss the latest programs for helping felines control their population. It's going to be a hard sell, but as the populations of humans and animals swell on the planet, we're all going to have to do our part.

There go Peter and the lovely Eleanor with our bags. I suppose I should follow along like a good kitty. I can sightsee once we're checked into our hotel.

Now who is that little pixie with the fire in her eyes? My goodness, she's handing out orders like a drill ser-

geant. And she has a whole troop to do her bidding. Dig those khaki shorts and those utilitarian hiking boots. All she needs is a pith helmet and she can sally forth into the desert in search of Dr. Livingston. But she is cute as a button.

Normally I go for the taller model humanette, but there's something about Miss Explorer that just makes me want to watch her. It's her determination. I can almost smell it. She's here on a mission, and nothing is going to stand in her way. I think I'll sidle over, do a little eavesdropping and see what she's up to.

Hmm. She's an anthropologist, and she's brought enough equipment to examine the tombs of the pharaohs. I just love women who dig up bones. That's sort of my job—digging up bones and clues and anything else that helps solve a mystery.

So she's looking for a lost civilization. Interesting, and not just to me. There's a man behind that pillar who's just as curious about Miss Explorer as I am. In fact, I'd say he's even more interested.

My, my. This man reminds me of nothing if not a hawk. And Miss Explorer seems to be his chosen meal. He's watching her as if he's about to dive down and attack at any moment.

At last she's got all her stuff together, and all those people who seem to be with her. There must be five people in her party, and from the looks of them, they all work outdoors. They're moving to the bus to go into town. Good. The man who was watching her is going in the opposite direction. Perhaps he was just a pickpocket.

Nah! I'd be willing to bet my elegant black hide that

he's not a common thief. The way he was watching Miss Explorer sort of made my hide itch.

I guess the only noble thing to do is get on the bus with Miss Explorer and head into town. Peter and Eleanor are staying at the Abbula, the ritziest hotel in town. I can find them there in time for dinner.

You know, I love this place. I can stroll around and no one pays the least bit of attention to me. There are cats everywhere. Some really hot little purr-furs, too. It's a little-known fact, but Cleopatra was a cat in a former life. That's when she learned to become such a seductress. She had a definite appreciation for her feline nature, and boy, did Mark Antony learn about it the hard way! I see one long, elegant black puss that might have a bit of the Cleopatra bloodline in her veins. But I have to behave. My heart belongs to the beautiful Clotilde, and I would never betray her trust.

I'm on the bus and settled just beneath the feet of the intrepid female explorer. The other members of her crew are calling her Beth. Now that's a nice sensible name. I'll just have to keep tabs on her for a little while to make sure that man from the airport isn't following her.

Eleanor and Peter will be worried, but I'll be back with them by dinnertime—and that's one promise I intend to keep. The last time they took me abroad and I disappeared in Ireland, they said they were never taking me out of the country again. I can't screw up my second chance at international travel, or they really won't let me out of Washington.

BETH BRADSHAW felt as if her body was on the verge of rebellion. She was exhausted. It had taken all of her energy to get her band of archaeologists and anthropologists onto the plane in New York and down in Alexandria. It was only when the jet had begun its descent and she'd looked out the window and seen the jewel of the Mediterranean shimmering like a blue opal beneath her that she realized she was actually about to land in Egypt. After months and months of planning, the real adventure was about to begin.

As the bus lumbered through the crowded streets of the city, Beth looked out the window at the passing sights. It was as if she was in a dream. The streets were full of men and women in the flowing robes of the Middle Eastern culture, though there were a few in western garb. Dark eyes gazed back at hers with mixed expressions of interest, curiosity and mild amusement.

And cats were all over the place.

She felt something brush against her feet and leaned down to discover a big black feline purring against her ankles.

She sighed. She wasn't particularly fond of cats. She was more a dog person. Cats had a streak of arrogance that left her feeling cool toward them. Dogs were always glad for a pat and some attention. Sort of like herself. Yep, she was definitely a dog person, while her best friend and self-appointed sister, Amelia, was the cat person.

"Beth, I thought our guide was going to meet us in the airport."

She looked up to find John Gilmore standing over her. She was already exhausted and John was an energy drain. No matter what was happening, he always found fault and something to worry about obsessively. "The guide knows the hotel we're staying at. I'm sure he'll find us there."

"But he said he was going to meet us in the airport. It upsets me that he didn't show. We're going deep into the desert with this man. We have to be able to trust him. Is he reliable?"

It was a question Beth had asked herself, but as she looked around the bus and saw that all her employees were listening, she knew she had to show absolute faith in the missing Omar Dukhan—even if she wanted to string him up for failing to live up to his word.

"Mr. Dukhan has an impeccable reputation as a guide. I'm sure there's a reason he didn't meet us in the airport. Once I talk to him, I'm certain I'll be satisfied with his explanation."

"And if you're not?" John asked.

"Then I'll find another guide." She looked around, meeting the eyes of the four other members of her crew. "I won't risk your lives or mine with someone I can't rely on." She forced a smile. "Many of you have worked for me before. I believe you call me Mama Beth behind my back, because I tend to mother my crew." She lifted an eyebrow and waited for the denials that didn't come. "Good. You know I'll take care of everything." She refocused on John. "I'll handle it, okay? Please don't worry anymore about it."

She watched as he returned to his seat, his face drawn with worry. He fretted over the smallest things, but he was the very best excavator she'd ever worked with. And he was a top-notch anthropologist, too. He would be invaluable in helping to establish the culture of the secret city—when she found it.

For a moment she allowed herself to slip into the dream. She was standing in the middle of a temple with an obelisk that depicted Ra, the sun god worshiped in ancient Egypt for thousands of years.

Beside the obelisk was a limestone statue of an exotic creature—a lovely feminine form with the head of a cat. Con, the mythic goddess, queen of a very secret cult.

Many Egyptologists believed that Con was a legend, as were so many of the gods and goddesses in ancient civilizations. But Beth knew better. Con had been a living, breathing woman, and she'd wielded tremendous power because of her special gift. She was a seer, a woman who had the power to view the future. And Beth believed—and intended to prove—that Con had lived in the Libyan Desert with her female followers, a tribe of women with the legendary skills of the Amazons and the added gift of second sight, a talent they'd used to manipulate the future.

As always, her heart began to race with the idea of finding the village that everyone else said was fiction.

"It's there," Beth whispered to herself. "It's there and I'm going to find it."

And become world-famous as a researcher and anthropologist, to boot, she added in her thoughts.

"Must be a nice fantasy you're having," Mauve Parker said as she plopped into the seat beside Beth, wiping sweat from beneath her bangs. "Doubtless about someplace cool with lots of shady trees. Why is it that ancient civilizations always seemed to thrive in hot, dry climates where there aren't any trees?''

Beth laughed easily. ''Only a girl from Alabama would miss trees. Anyway, my fantasy is right here in Egypt. We're in the secret village, and there's a temple where the inhabitants worshiped Ra and Con.''

''Sounds nice, but sort of ordinary,'' Mauve teased.

''Everything is *perfectly* preserved.'' Beth said the last with big eyes and emphasis.

''Once we find it and reveal it, that won't be the case for long,'' Mauve said with a touch of bitterness.

''I know. Once we reveal the site, it becomes part of the public domain. It won't be our private discovery. But we'll have it all to ourselves for a while.''

''Long enough to do our research and prepare our papers, right?'' Mauve asked.

''Right,'' Beth said.

''Can I ask a question?'' Mauve put a hand on Beth's knee.

''Sure.''

''You never said where you got the financial backing for this trip. It's not like you to keep secrets, Beth. Is there a reason you're not telling?''

There was a very good reason. The man who'd agreed to pick up the tab for the expedition had insisted on absolute privacy. He had made it very clear that he would withdraw all funding if he were ever linked to the project.

''Competition.'' Beth finally said as her gaze strayed to John Gilmore.

''Gilmore? He can't hold a candle to you,'' Mauve said. ''He's an excellent detail man and he's good at interpreting the minutiae, but John can't see the big picture. He's always going to be second-in-command. If not to you, then to someone else."

"He doesn't see it that way," Beth said.

"He wouldn't. We're just lucky to have him on the diving end of it. Hard to believe someone who counts rubber bands and paper clips like an accountant is so fearless underwater."

"True." Beth had learned long ago that conflicting character traits couldn't always be explained. She'd given up trying.

"What do you think you'll find in the submerged cities in the Mediterranean?"

"The clues that will lead us to the City of Con." She spoke so matter-of-factly that her friend was apparently shocked.

"Beth, you're staking your career on this."

"I know," Beth said a lot more calmly than she felt.

"What if we don't find the city?"

"I can always go back to the States and continue my research in Arizona."

"But—"

"But everyone will know I failed?" Beth said. She'd rehearsed this answer a million times. "I guess I finally decided that it was better for people to know I'd failed than for me to know I'd never tried."

Mauve's eyebrows arched. "You've really changed. You used to play it so safe. Now you're this bold adventurer."

Beth's laughter was soft and pleasant. "Hardly. I'm thirty-two, Mauve. We both are. If we're going to make our mark, we have to do it now. In another ten years, we may not be able to hold up physically to the rigors of this kind of search.''

"So true," Mauve said.

Beth knew they were both thinking of several of their colleagues who'd had to retire from the field and assume teaching positions. The grueling life of living in tents in heat and freezing temperatures, and the physical labor required eventually took a toll on everyone in the field.

"When do we head out on the water?" Mauve asked eagerly.

"First thing tomorrow. I want to do the underwater exploration in no more than three days and then head into the desert.''

Mauve nodded. "Your will is my command," she said jokingly, then stood up as the bus stopped in front of an elegant and ancient hotel.

OMAR DUKHAN watched the arrival of the archaeologists from the lobby of the hotel. He knew who he was looking for—he'd seen them in the airport. And he didn't like what he saw.

Beth Bradshaw certainly wasn't the woman he thought she'd be. First of all, she was petite, with shiny mahogany hair and brown eyes, and she looked far too delicate to be leading a major dig. At first glance, he'd assumed she was someone's daughter!

He'd also noted the equipment that had come with the crew. It was state-of-the-art and brand-new. Someone had spent a lot of money on this trip. This was a serious effort, not some college adventure funded by grants.

It all added up to trouble for him.

He watched as Beth organized the unloading of the equipment, and took in the different attitudes of her crew members. He noted immediately the stiff spine of the man. He also saw the friendship in the eyes of the woman with the bangs. She would be Beth's ally.

Omar made sure that he stayed out of sight as the crew registered and had the bellman load up their bags. It was only when Beth stepped into the center of the lobby and began to slowly scan the vast room that he stepped out from behind the palm tree where he'd remained secluded.

"Miss Bradshaw," he said, walking forward and extending his hand. "I was delayed earlier. A problem with arranging for the camels."

"Not a serious problem, I hope," she said, worry evident in her eyes.

He took her hand and felt the smallest pulse of… something. She was a vital woman—he could feel it in her handshake. She was very much like Leah, a mare he'd chosen for his own. Leah was deceptive, standing patiently outside his tent for hours. But once he was on her back, she was the wind. She had a spirit she felt no need to demonstrate—until it was needed.

"No, not a serious problem. Everything has been taken care of." He held her hand a fraction of a moment longer than necessary. She withdrew her own hand slowly, her gaze locked with his.

"Mr. Dukhan," she said, a slight flush touching her fair skin. "I was a little worried."

"I apologize," he said, picking up her hand again and bringing it to his lips. He lowered his head in respect as he kissed the back of her hand lightly in the European style.

When he looked up, he saw that his gesture had done little to reassure Beth Bradshaw. The flush had deepened and her eyes were huge.

"It's okay," she said, again pulling her hand out of his grasp. "Everything is fine now?"

"Absolutely. Your expedition will go off without a hitch. Are you still planning on following the original path?" He saw that she was instantly more comfortable once she was talking about her work.

"Tomorrow morning we're diving into the ruined cities that were recently discovered off the coast."

"Ah, the scientists believe that an earthquake may have sent the cities tumbling into the sea," he said, watching the surprise cross her face at his knowledge.

"Yes. I guess it was a big story in all the newspapers."

"Egypt is a land where the past is often of more interest than the present. Or the future," he said, unable to keep a hint of harshness out of his voice. "Most of my countrymen pay attention to archaeological finds. They will bring more tourists into our country. The economy will grow."

"I see," Beth said.

"Do you?" he asked, stepping closer to her. Did she have any idea what would really happen to his land, his people, if she should make a major archaeological find? He doubted it, and he also doubted that she would care.

"Tomorrow we'll make the dives," Beth said, faltering only slightly. "Once we conclude that, we'll begin the overland trek. From the clues I've discovered, I think we'll be heading somewhere close to the oasis, as I said in my correspondence to you.''

''Fine,'' Omar said. ''Then I will meet you here tomorrow evening.''

''Thank you,'' Beth said.

Omar turned quickly, his desert robe flowing around his legs, and walked into the night. He had gone several blocks before he realized he wasn't certain of his destination. More than anything he wanted to get back to the desert, back to his people, his way of life. He hated the city. And he hated the chaos that Beth Bradshaw and her colleagues were so determined to bring to his people.

She would never find the City of Con. For centuries he and his tribe had protected the secret. It was their heritage, their place to worship and to revere their ancestors. The secrets of Con were theirs to protect against the prying fingers of the world. Omar accepted what it meant to be the leader of his people. He would protect them no matter the cost. Beth Bradshaw was a woman who ignited his blood, but she was also a woman who would have to fail.

Chapter Two

Beth followed the bellhop to her room, her face still suffused with heat. The encounter with Omar Dukhan was not what she'd anticipated. She'd expected a rugged man, a man of the desert. Omar was so much more than that. In his dark eyes she'd seen the fiery heat of the desert and the swirl of a storm.

She'd also seen something darker, something that made her heart race and her palms sweat.

She tipped the bellhop and closed her door, then leaned against it. Her attraction to the guide was unexpected, but she'd always been able to control herself. There had been other attractive men in her life, and she'd never found herself leaning against a door, knees like putty.

She walked to the bed and began to unpack a bag. She was behaving like a fool. So she felt desire for Omar Dukhan. Big deal. He was a handsome man. That wasn't what was really bothering her.

She thought back to the conversation. Although he was a hired hand, he had treated her as if he was in charge. That bothered her.

There was something else, though. She thought about

it as she laid out her sleeveless blouses and shorts. There had been an edge of danger about the man. For everything that he said, there were a million things unsaid. She realized, smiling at her imagination, that she could easily view him as a spy.

"Bond. James Bond," she said out loud, mocking herself.

Her ability to laugh at herself helped ease the disquiet she felt. She went to the telephone and sat, knowing that patience would be required to get a call through to the United States.

She'd left Arizona without a word to Amelia Corbet or Amelia's parents, Luther and Susan. The Corbets had been Beth's family for the past fifteen years, and she wanted to make sure they knew where she was and that she was safe. She hadn't called them because she was afraid that, in their attempt to protect her, they might fuel her own self-doubt in her ability to bring off this expedition. The Corbets had supported her in every aspect of her work, but they also felt a duty to shelter her from danger and disappointment. Now, though, Beth was too deeply engaged in the trip to pull back. It was time to let them know where she was.

As she dialed Amelia's number in New York, she felt once again the thrill of her undertaking. She was actually on an adventure. She was doing something that Amelia would do.

To her disappointment, when the call finally went through, she got Amelia's answering machine. According to the message, Beth's best friend and "sister" was out of town for a few days to meet with a client in Tokyo.

Amelia worked for a high-powered public-relations firm, and her work took her all over the globe and into the most interesting situations.

Beth hung up without leaving a message. She wanted to tell *Amelia* about her expedition, not her machine. She wanted the satisfaction of hearing Amelia's gasp of surprise when she told her she was in Alexandria, Egypt, on a trip that could gain her the kind of recognition in her field that many only dreamed about.

Glancing at her watch, she stood up. She was due to meet her team in the dining room. She'd organized an early dinner, a bit of walking around, then an early bedtime. Tomorrow would be a long, grueling day, even for those who were not diving. For herself, John and four others, it was going to be an exhausting day.

She went downstairs and entered the hotel restaurant. At the happy looks on the faces of her co-workers, she felt her shoulders relax. Everything was going to be fine. They were all going to receive the recognition for which they had worked so hard.

So, Miss Explorer enters the dining room. I can't hang around for long. I have a very important date with something fresh and delicious from the Mediterranean and Peter and Eleanor. Besides, everything looks fine here.

The guy at the airport was obviously her guide. He didn't make his presence known because he wanted to check out her party before he decided to take them into the desert. I can see his point—I wouldn't want to be stranded in the sand with a herd of whiners. On the other hand, I don't really think that lurking behind a pillar and spying on someone is the way to behave, either.

There's something about this Omar Dukhan that makes me want to keep him under close surveillance. But this isn't my case. I'm not here to work. I'm on vacation. Even I need a break from the pressures of solving mysteries every now and again.

Beth Bradshaw has everything under control. I think I can safely head for the Abbula Hotel and my reserved room. I'll just make a quick sweep of the hotel rooms here while all the scientists are in the dining room. One last quick check before I trundle out into the night.

Mauve's room seems fine. A little trip down the hall, and the other three rooms are good. Silent as tombs, no pun intended.

Now back to John's room, right beside Beth's. I'll creep in for just a moment. I'm a little curious about him, too. If he's such a worrywart, why'd he come on this trip?

Wait. What's that? Someone is in his room. Listen. What's that noise? It sounds like a gas valve or air or—someone is letting the air out of his diving tank.

I'll put an end to this. Wham! My body slamming into the door has frightened him. He's running across the room and out the window into the night. He's fast, whoever he is. Before I can even get to the window, he's cleared the wall around the hotel garden and disappeared.

Now why would someone break into a room to let the air out of a diving tank?

Maybe Miss Explorer could use a few more hours of watching. I'm not sure what's going on here, but I'm getting a really bad feeling. Cats have always had psychic abilities. That, too, is a little-known fact. We're very attuned to use of the sixth sense. In all the best ways, of course. And my intuition is telling me to stay close to Miss Explorer tonight.

Criminy. I guess I'll have to rush over to the Abbula Hotel, eat a bite with Peter and Eleanor, and then get back over here to make sure no one bothers Beth.

OMAR FOUND HIMSELF standing in front of the high-rise building that contained his brother's development firm. Dukhan Enterprises was one of Egypt's most prestigious firms. Known for innovative architecture and global outlook, the company was a big part of the changing face of Egypt.

Omar thought of his brother, and his mouth tightened. Harad Dukhan insisted he was leading Egypt forward into the future. A brighter future. Omar wasn't so sure.

He looked up at the high rise. It was a beautiful building, all white limestone and glass. In any other city it would have been a marvel.

In Alexandria, it was an eyesore.

He squared his shoulders and went to the main door, where an armed security guard looked at him with a wary eye.

"Can I help you, sir?"

Omar knew that his desert robes had aroused the guard's suspicions. Many of the nomadic desert people in Egypt were opposed to what they considered westernization. Like Omar, some viewed Harad Dukhan as a man who'd climbed into bed with the capitalists. Un-

like Omar, these people didn't love Harad Dukhan.
Some of them wanted to kill him.

"Is Harad still at work? I'm his brother."

The guard spoke into a telephone, and in a moment
pushed buttons to open the door electronically. "Tenth
floor," he said.

Omar nodded. It had been at least five years since
he'd stepped foot on his brother's property. Five years
since he'd seen his brother. He rode the elevator up
and stepped into an elaborate office. Against the wall,
backlit by the beauty of the city, his brother sat at a
desk. Very slowly he leaned forward.

"Omar," Harad said with some surprise. "You
haven't been to Alexandria in over five years. What's
wrong?"

"I need a favor," Omar said. He gave no indication
how glad he was to see his brother or how much it cost
him to ask for help. They had parted bitterly, with
harsh words on both sides. To his relief, he saw that
Harad was not going to mention the argument that had
caused such a rift between them.

"What can I do?" Harad asked.

"There's an expedition set up to search for the City
of Con." He saw his brother flinch. So Harad still, at
least, had some affection for his desert roots, for the
things his nomadic people held close. For the place
where their mother had been buried.

"There have been other expeditions. None of them
have succeeded," Harad said carefully.

"This woman, Beth Bradshaw, she's different."

Instead of questioning Omar, Harad simply nodded.
"What can I do to help my brother?"

"Find out who's backing her. If we can get the money withdrawn, she'll have no choice but to go home." Omar held on to his composure, but it was hard. Like old times, Harad was there for him.

"I can try to find that information." Harad got to his feet slowly. "Will you have dinner with me?"

Omar almost said no, then he hesitated. "We're as different as the lion and the camel. Can we share a meal without one getting eaten by the other?"

Harad's smile was amused but sad. "Perhaps for one meal the lion can put aside his claws and teeth. I've missed you, brother." He stepped forward and took his brother's elbow. "You've lost weight, gotten hard, like the desert people."

"Like *our* people, Harad." Omar looked around the elegantly appointed office. "This is not where you belong. We're free people. Nomads of the desert."

Harad only squeezed Omar's arm more tightly. "You've made your choice, brother. I don't intend to try and talk you into putting your university education to use. Please, don't try to talk me out of my chosen life."

Omar nodded. "For tonight," he said.

Harad smiled. "Shall we go someplace quiet where we can talk, or noisy where we can laugh?"

Omar's lean face broke into a grin. "Noisy. With good food and beautiful women." There was one woman he definitely wanted out of his mind, and the distractions of some of his brother's beautiful friends would be the perfect way to erase Beth Bradshaw.

"Done," Harad said, and picked up his neatly folded suit jacket. "I'm glad to see you, Omar. Very glad."

They walked out of the building together and headed toward the waterfront, where the restaurants were busy and the sound of laughter rang out over the water.

BETH SAT UP in bed, her heart pounding. It took several seconds for her to realize that her terror came from a nightmare, not from any real threat. In the time it took her to calm her fears, she recognized the hotel room, felt again the thrill of actually being in Egypt.

Taking deep breaths, she got out of bed and walked to the French doors that opened to the balcony. They were slightly open, allowing the breeze to flutter the sheer curtains. She was on the second floor of the old hotel, and her room looked out over a beautiful garden.

Slipping a robe over her short cotton nightshirt, she walked out onto the balcony and into a night that smelled of saltwater and unfamiliar spices. She'd asked the concierge in the hotel about the scent, and he'd told her it was tumeric and cumin, spices that had once been like gold in the East-West trade market.

She went to the railing and placed her hands on it, allowing her eyes to close and her body to fill with the scents and sounds around her. Alexandria. Jewel of the Mediterranean. The city had been a cultural and trading center of the Greek and Roman empires. Cleopatra had reigned from here, and had loved both Julius Caesar and Mark Antony.

She walked to the end of the balcony and almost screamed when a black shadow darted out of a chair. "Cat," she said, a hand at her throat. "You frightened the life out of me." A big black cat, he looked exactly like the one that had been on the bus with her. But there were a million cats in Egypt, and a lot of them were black. Surely it wasn't the same one.

"Meow."

The cat didn't seem in an apologetic mood, but then, cats never apologized.

"You could at least pretend," she said, taking the seat the cat had vacated.

To her surprise, the cat flopped over on his back at her feet, a low, pleading meow escaping his throat.

"Well, okay, you're forgiven," she said, feeling only a little foolish for talking to the cat.

As if he understood, the cat jumped onto her lap with a quickness and agility that was truly amazing. She stroked his head and was rewarded with a purr.

"I guess cats aren't so bad," she said, tickling him under the chin. "But don't you belong to someone?"

He continued to purr, settling on her lap as she stroked him. Beyond the wall of the garden were the sounds of a large city.

Beth settled back into the chair. Having the cat on her lap gave her a sense of contentment. She was completely in darkness while around her the city pulsed with life. This was the role she knew so well, the one she'd played most of her life, that of observer. In her work she examined the artifacts of the past and from them wove the pattern of daily life. She knew the routine of the Indian women of the Southwest, the day-to-day struggle to feed a family and maintain life in an arid climate.

By examining those ancient remains, she could reconstruct a world that no longer existed. And it was a world often richer and more real than her own world.

In the shards of pottery, she found evidence of wedding feasts and the celebration of everyday life. The long-dead people she studied were filled with emotion and the visible bonds of family. So far, other than the Corbets, she hadn't found any of those emotional links.

She knew she should go back to bed, but the remnants of the bad dream kept her from attempting to go back to sleep.

She heard the outer gate of the garden creak open, and she leaned forward to catch a glimpse of the person coming in so late at night. A lone man walked into the garden with purpose and caught her attention even when she didn't intend to stare. Halfway across the garden, he stopped.

He wore the flowing robes of the desert, and even in the semidarkness she could see that he stood tall and proud. Something about him was vaguely familiar, and she felt a strange increase in her pulse.

She couldn't see his features, but she was certain she'd seen him before.

The guide! It was Omar Dukhan. He was standing in the garden looking up at her room.

Beth eased back into the chair so that she would be completely hidden from his view. The cat slipped from her lap and walked to the balcony railing. He stood with his tail twitching slightly, as if he, too, knew the identity of the man in the garden.

Beth watched in fascination as Omar continued toward the hotel, disappearing beneath her balcony as he approached the entrance. He was obviously staying in the hotel, too.

She started to call the cat to her when she heard a

noise on the balcony next to her. The sound came from John Gilmore's room, and she leaned out over the balcony to see what was going on.

John stood at the railing, watching as Omar entered the hotel. He remained a moment longer and then went back inside his room.

The cat ran into her room and began scratching at the door to the hall. She moved to the door and listened carefully before opening it a crack. John stepped from his room into the hallway, turned his head in both directions and then hurried toward the stairs that led to the first floor.

Even though she wore her nightgown and robe, Beth slipped into the hallway and began to follow John. The cat was at her side and gave her a sense of security that she knew was silly. He was only a cat, but his presence did help.

The hotel hallway was empty, filled with the silence of early morning. She started down the stairs and felt something tug at her gown. Surprised, she turned around to find the cat hooking his right paw into the lace of her nightshirt and holding firm.

As soon as she stopped, he darted in front of her and took the lead, stopping at the bottom of the stairs and peeking around the corner. He was acting as if he knew what they were doing—spying on John Gilmore and the intense Omar Dukhan.

The cat gave a low growl, which Beth took to mean that she should be very quiet. She eased up beside him and immediately saw the two men in conversation in the empty lobby.

The look on Omar's face was inscrutable. He lis-

tened as John talked with great passion. Beth was too
far away from the men to hear what they were saying.
She glanced around the room, searching for a place that
would conceal her while still allowing her to eaves-
drop. There was nothing except a sofa near the men.
She'd have to cross fifty feet of open floor to get to it.
Impossible.

The cat patted her knee once with his paw and then
darted across the room. He made a beeline for the sofa
and slipped beneath it without either man noticing him.

Great! The cat could hear the conversation, but since
he didn't talk, he couldn't relay what had been said.
Beth fumed as she hid at the foot of the stairs. She
didn't like the idea of John Gilmore and Omar Dukhan
meeting in secret.

Well, not exactly in secret, but pretty darn close. It
was three in the morning. John had obviously been
waiting on the balcony for Omar to return. Their meeting appeared to have had been prearranged. And that
didn't sit well with Beth.

Watching the two men, she saw that whatever Omar
Dukhan might be feeling, he didn't show a thing. He
only listened and gave the occasional monosyllabic re-
ply.

John, on the other hand, was red-faced, his hands
gesticulating wildly. John's temper was one of his most
serious drawbacks as a leader. When a crew member
messed up, that was the time he or she needed the most
support. John's response was always biting anger and
cruel remarks, which destroyed a crew's desire to work.

It seemed that John was angry with Omar, but about
what? Beth felt her skin tingle and dance. The idea that

there was some sort of pact between the two was unnerving. She didn't trust either of them. That was what it boiled down to. A total lack of trust.

John abruptly turned away from Omar and started toward the stairs. Beth, caught unprepared, scampered back up the stairs and barely made it into her room before she heard John's step in the second-floor hallway. But she was panting more with emotion than exertion as she sat down on her bed.

John walked past her room, entered his own and closed the door. Beth heard a faint scratching at her door and opened it. The black cat stood there, tail twitching. He brushed past her and leaped onto the bed, settling in among the pillows.

"Meow," he said softly, curling around again in an invitation for her to come to bed.

"Okay," she said. There was nothing else she could do. As much as she wanted to charge into John's room and demand to know what he was up to, she knew he wouldn't tell her. The only thing to do was bide her time and figure it out later. But figure it out she would. Until then, she'd double-check every arrangement Omar Dukhan made on her behalf.

And search for another guide.

I ONLY CAUGHT the tail end of the conversation between Desert Hawk and John Gilmore, but it wasn't a happy exchange. Obviously John had accused Hawk of something, Hawk had denied it, and then hot words had flown. All from the mouth of John. Hawkman hardly said a word.

I'm wondering if John was huffy about Omar's fail-

*ing to meet them in the airport, or if he's already dis-
covered that his air tank has been tampered with. Or
maybe there's something else going on. How did John
know that Omar would be coming in through the garden gate? Did they have a rendezvous time arranged?*

*There are many questions to be answered, but right
now this kitty needs some shut-eye. Dinner at the Abbula was a little too rich. Eleanor ordered for me, and
then allowed me to sample all the goodies they had left
over. Women! They know that the way to a cat's heart
is through his stomach. But mine is a little bloated. Ah,
I remember the good old days when I could eat five
platefuls of food and never have a moment of regret.*

*This aging business is getting to be a little annoying.
If I'm going to keep my svelte feline figure, I'm going
to have to cut down on the rich food or beef up the old
exercise regime.*

*For now, though, I'm in bed with a very sexy little
anthropologist. I'll bet she would be excellent at some
under-the-sheet explorations. Ah, some man is going to
be very, very lucky when she finally settles on him.*

Until tomorrow!

Chapter Three

Beth sat at the breakfast table, a fresh crusty roll and a cup of coffee in front of her, when she saw Omar walk into the room.

His gaze sought hers instantly and he came toward her.

"Shall I accompany you on this part of your exploration?" he asked.

Beth hadn't anticipated that the desert guide would be interested in diving.

"You're welcome to come if you want," she said, studying him for any reaction. "It isn't necessary, you know."

His dark eyes held hers. "The sunken cities are relatively unexplored. I've read about them, and I'd like to see them."

"Do you dive?" Beth was surprised and couldn't hide it.

Omar's smile was cool and amused. "Is it so hard to believe that a man of the desert might be accomplished in scuba diving?"

"Well, yes," Beth said. "There isn't a whole lot of opportunity to dive in the desert. I didn't mean it as a slight. I wouldn't expect someone who grew up in New York City to know how to water-ski, either.''

"Point taken," he said, the hardness of his face relaxing a little.

The waiter came and set a cup of coffee in front of Omar.

"Do you mind?" Omar asked.

"Please, join me," Beth said. She hadn't expected to see Omar so early, and she certainly hadn't expected to have breakfast with him. "How are the plans for the overland trip going? Did you secure more camels?"

"Everything is in order," he assured her. "Please, don't worry. I've led many Americans into the desert and brought all of them back safely."

"Have you ever been on an archaeological exploration before?" Beth asked.

Omar hesitated, his dark eyes steady as he stared at her. "Yes."

"Did you enjoy it?"

"No." He sipped his coffee, finally breaking eye contact.

"Why not?"

He hesitated. "Perhaps you can't understand this, but I'll tell you, anyway. When foreigners come into my land to examine and explore, it's like locusts coming to rob my people of their heritage. Foreign scientists discover valuable artifacts, and they steal them for foreign museums or worse, private collections. Egypt is robbed of her past."

"I'm not interested in taking anything out of Egypt," Beth said quickly. "Everything will remain here."

"Perhaps you mean that when you say it, but you have no control over the people who will follow you. You cannot guarantee there won't be political deals made by the leaders of my country and others. Many men believe that trading the past for the future is acceptable. I don't happen to share that belief."

Beth's hand clenched around her butter knife. "Omar, if we can find the City of Con, it would bring a lot of worldwide attention to Egypt. Con, I believe, was a flesh-and-blood woman and a seer who ruled with as much power as any of the pharaohs. It would change history."

His dark eyes were bright with emotion. "Perhaps Egypt doesn't want the world's attention. Perhaps we wish to keep our history to ourselves. I'm not so certain that it's our responsibility to change the world's view."

Beth started to argue, but she bit back her words. Omar wasn't going to be convinced by anything she said, and in some ways she understood him. "I can only tell you that I intend to explore the city with the greatest respect. I'll work in full cooperation with your government and do everything I can to make sure all sites are protected for your people."

For a brief moment his eyes softened. "I'm sure you will try, Beth Bradshaw."

"Your government has given me permission—"

"It isn't the government that you should be worried about," Omar interrupted. He finished his coffee and abruptly stood up. "I'll meet you on the boat."

"It's the—"

"*Memphis,*" he finished for her. "I know."

"How did you..." She didn't finish the question.

She knew how he knew. John Gilmore had told him. "Omar," she called to him as he started through the restaurant.

He stopped and turned around, but didn't approach the table.

She stood up and went to him. "What were you and John talking about last night in the lobby?"

She saw surprise flicker across his face.

"Your co-worker felt it necessary to explain to me that I should have been at the airport, that I was remiss in my duties and insubordinate to my employer. He also made an allegation against me. One that I refuted."

Beth felt little sparks of heat run up her neck and into her cheeks. "It isn't John's place to do that."

"I listened to him."

"John has nothing to do with any of the arrangements. He's a paid hand on this expedition. What did he accuse you of?"

"I'll keep in mind that you are the leader of this trip," Omar said. "The other is insignificant." He left the restaurant with a long, purposeful stride, brushing past Mauve as she came in.

Mauve arched her eyebrows at Beth and hurried to the table where the empty coffee cup told the story of breakfast. "My, oh, my, you do work fast," Mauve said wickedly. "Was it breakfast after aerobics or just a little preliminary feast before doing some mattress maneuvers?"

Beth couldn't help but laugh, even though Mauve's teasing accusations made her slightly uncomfortable. It was hard to be around Omar for any length of time without feeling desire. He was a very sexy man. But desire had no place on this expedition.

"Omar's going on the dive with us," Beth said. "He knows how to dive and he's interested in the sunken cities."

"Terrific," Mauve said. "I'm very interested in seeing what he's hiding under those flowing robes."

Beth laughed despite herself. "You are a wicked girl," she said to her friend.

"Wicked but honest. You're curious, too, aren't you? Unless you've already had a little preview," Mauve teased.

"Get your mind out of the bedroom and onto your work," Beth said, finishing her roll and rising from the table. "I'll meet everyone at the boat. I want to make sure all the equipment is loaded."

WELL, I'VE LEARNED two valuable lessons today. The hard rolls served for breakfast may satisfy the humanoids, but not me. I want sausage or bacon or an omelet with shrimp and Parmesan cheese. Hard roll—yuck. Not even butter can make it palatable.

Probably of more importance is the second thing I've learned by hiding under Miss Explorer's table. Omar Dukhan hedged the truth. He and John Gilmore were not talking about the airport incident. John was actually accusing our fearless guide of tampering with the air tanks. Now that's interesting. Why would Gilmore jump to the conclusion that Omar had gone into his room and done that?

Diving tank. Boat. Water. I'd rather face lions and tigers and bears. I'd rather face the Wicked Witch of

*the West and all her flying monkeys. I'd even rather
face the Munchkins, though I don't want to hear them
sing, than get on another boat. But I'll be on the* Memphis *or my name isn't Familiar.*

*I don't trust Omar the desert guide, and I don't like
John Gilmore. I think Miss Explorer has put herself
behind the eight ball in this entire adventure. It's up
to me to see that nothing bad happens to her.*

OMAR HEFTED his diving tanks onto the deck of the
Memphis and then began to go over the other gear that
was already loaded. The expedition was professional
and expensive. He could only wonder again where
Beth Bradshaw had gotten the funding.

He had to hand it to her; she was not only smart,
she was prepared.

She was right on target, going to Herakleion, one of
the sunken cities, to look for specific directions to the
City of Con. It was in the coastal city that Con had
performed many of her most impressive feats. She had
predicted the coming of the Romans and the romance
between Cleopatra and Mark Antony. Con had warned
of the dangers of the liaison, but her warnings had gone
unheeded. Queen Cleopatra, the last of the Ptolemies,
had died by her own hand, a snake clutched to her
bosom. Alexandria, jewel of the Mediterranean, and
Egypt, the center of culture for the past century, were
forever changed.

And Con and her followers had taken to the desert,
hunted like dogs.

But Con and her followers had not been destroyed.
They had built a village where the world leaders often

sent emissaries to have dreams foretold and to buy a glimpse of the future.

Taking her gift of seeing the future, Con had gone into exile, but she was still very much a presence. So much so that legends began to spring up about her. Her name was whispered in all the halls of power. Assassins were sent to destroy her.

None succeeded.

Omar knew all this. He knew it was not just legend, but truth. He knew because he was descended from the lineage of Con. And he was the protector of her palace.

"Dukhan!"

Omar was pulled out of his reverie by the shout from the dock. He stood up and saw Beth Bradshaw and her party as they approached the boat. The man who'd hailed him was in the lead, John Gilmore.

"What are you doing here?" John asked him angrily.

Omar didn't bother to answer. He knew his lack of courtesy would infuriate the scientist, and he was right.

"Are you deaf, as well as stubborn?" John asked.

"John!" Beth's voice was sharp. "What do you think you're doing? Mr. Dukhan is my guest on this trip."

"Guest? He's hired help. And he went into my room last night and—"

"Choose your words carefully," Omar said in a deadly voice. "In my country, a man's honor is worth dying for."

John stared at Omar with open dislike.

"What's this about?" Beth demanded.

"Nothing," John said, looking away.

"John, Omar is a hired hand, but so are you," Beth said pointedly. "Now put aside whatever it is that's eating you or go back to the hotel. I don't have time for temper fits and rudeness."

She glanced once at Omar, and he saw the embarrassment in her eyes. She was ashamed of her countryman, and Omar felt a twinge of guilt for deliberately provoking the scientist. John Gilmore was such an easy mark, though.

John brushed past him, and Omar assisted the other members of Beth's party aboard. The site of the sunken city was fifteen miles off the coast, still in the Bay of Aboukir. Omar knew the craft Beth had rented would get them there in good time, and he looked out at the water, a beautiful aqua that promised adventure and a cool break from the heat that was already building.

As the boat left the dock, Omar kept his distance, aware of the surreptitious glances that the members of the crew cast his way. One of the women, a vibrant redhead, winked at him, and he flashed her a smile. But his gaze kept drifting back to Beth.

She wore a blue, one-piece swimsuit, which though conservative, showed off her figure. Her waist was tiny, and her hips swelled beneath it. Though she was short, her legs were tapered and beautifully proportioned. She was a lovely woman, with her dark hair sparkling in the sun.

He was watching her when he noticed the black cat sit down at her feet. There were thousands of black cats in Alexandria, but this one was…unique. He felt the cat's golden gaze on him, and he examined the feline. To his amusement the cat stood up and walked right to him. It jumped up on the seat beside him and with a deliberate action, hooked both front claws into the flesh of his thigh.

"Hey!" He was more startled than injured.

Everyone around stopped what they were doing and stared at him as he gently tried to disengage the cat. Unfortunately the animal only hooked his claws in farther and gave a low, warning growl.

Beth saw what was happening and hurried over. She carefully picked up the cat, unhooking the claws. The black devil began to purr in her arms and licked her chin.

"My goodness," Beth said, cradling the cat. "Are you okay?" she asked Omar.

"Fine," he said, rubbing his leg. He eyed the cat. "Is he yours?"

"He's been following me." Beth laughed when she realized how sinister that sounded. "Really, he has."

Omar found that he was smiling in amusement at her. There were many things about Beth Bradshaw that surprised and delighted him. She was supposed to be a cool, calm scientist, and here she was claiming that a stray cat was following her. "Since when?" he asked.

"Since the airport, and you can drop the condescension. It's the same cat, and he's been stuck to me like glue ever since I got into this country."

Omar studied the animal more closely. There had been a black cat in the airport, one that had given him the once-over. And there had been a black cat in the lobby of the hotel the evening before, hiding under some furniture. As he thought about it, the cat had seemed incredibly interested in the conversation he was having with John Gilmore.

"In my country," he said, "cats are worshiped. They roam wherever they like, but they hardly ever stalk tourists." He couldn't suppress the smile that teased the corners of his mouth.

"In my country, some people believe that black cats are the familiars—" She didn't get a chance to finish.

"Me-ow!" The cat leaped from her arms and landed on the seat beside Omar, who instinctively put his hands on his thighs to protect them from the cat's sharp claws.

"Me-ow!"

"Familiar?" Omar said carefully, though he could hardly believe the cat was trying to tell his name.

"Me-ow!" The cat nuzzled his leg, rubbing his head against the white robe with great relish.

Omar looked up at Beth. "I think that's his name."

"But that would be an American—"

"Me-ow!" Familiar lifted a paw and held it up. Tentatively Beth met his paw with her own hand. "Me-ow!" the cat proclaimed, swatting her palm with his claws sheathed.

"Incredible. He just gave me a high-five," Beth said.

"Incredible indeed," Omar said. He watched the cat intently. There was something odd about this one. He'd known and loved cats all his life, but he'd never seen a cat who could so clearly communicate with humans.

John Gilmore sauntered up to Beth and Omar. "So the two of you are adopting a stray cat," he said with one corner of his mouth twisted. "How cute. I'm just wondering if we're here for an archaeological expedition or as emissaries of the Humane Society.''

Omar's fist clenched, though he made sure that no other part of his body registered his anger. Beside him, Beth, too, tensed.

"If you're so overly worried about our expedition, why aren't you suited up for the dive?" Beth asked with a measure of calm that Omar could only admire. She was a woman who'd learned to govern her emotions and to sharpen her tongue for use as a weapon. What she lacked in physical size, she made up for in spirit and intelligence.

"I could ask you the same," John countered. "Him, too."

"You could, but you aren't in charge of this expedition. I am," Beth said evenly. "You don't have to worry your pretty little head about any of the decisions that need to be made. That's my job." Her tone suddenly hardened. "Now suit up and prepare to dive."

Omar watched as John's face suffused with blood. Beth had angered him deliberately. He felt a tiny smile tug at the corners of his mouth. Sometimes words were far more effective than fists.

John abruptly wheeled around and went to put on his diving gear. Mauve sauntered up to Beth. "That wasn't particularly smart. You're going down in the sea with him."

"John is annoying, but once we get to work, he's a professional," Beth said.

"I hope you're right," Mauve said. "I'd feel better if I were going down there with you."

Beth shook her head. "I need you on top here. You can run the equipment better than anyone."

"I'll be there with you," Omar said, and both women turned to him. "As your guide, I'll be at your back at all times."

He saw the slight tremor pass through Beth, and he couldn't help but wonder if the reaction was to the hint of a threat his words induced, or the image of him standing behind her, protecting her from anyone who dared threaten. He wasn't sure exactly which he preferred.

Chapter Four

"Now, we all know what we're looking for?" Beth asked as she stood on the deck of the boat with the four members of the crew who were diving with her. Omar stood slightly behind her, but she was more than aware of his presence. She shot a glance at Mauve, who was staring blatantly at Omar's sculpted chest and stomach, the lean and sinewy legs that emerged from the bottom of his conservative swim trunks. She'd always disliked the small briefs-style suits some men favored, much preferring the boxer-shorts style.

And in Omar's case, she was more than a little interested in the man who wore them.

At the sound of Mauve clearing her throat, loudly, Beth brought her attention back to the group who stood in the hot Egyptian sun waiting for her to continue. Mauve's wicked grin almost made her choke. She flushed but got a grip on her thoughts.

"If my hypothesis is correct, we should find a temple built to Con in Herakleion. In the temple there should be hieroglyphics that will reveal the exact location of the lost city.

"If it exists," John said.

Anger made Beth whirl to look at him, but before she spoke she'd already governed her temper. "John, we all know that we're here to explore my personal *hypothesis*. You knew that when you signed on. Creating doubt in the project isn't helpful, and if it continues, I will send you back to the States."

"A professional always doubts." He lifted his chin and glanced at the other members of the dive team.

Beth noticed that only two of them met John's glance—Ray and Judy—the two who doubted her the most. John was always a pain in the butt, but he was sometimes helpful. She made a note to question Ray and Judy closely after they made the dive. Their doubt could prevent them from seeing a clue.

"Doubt can be effective, but not nearly as much as belief," Beth countered. "I believe in the lost City of Con. I believe in the woman who became a goddess. And I believe she had the ability of second sight. Those of you who don't believe the same, just keep an open mind and we'll gather our facts and let the evidence prove or disprove my theory."

She nodded and began to adjust her diving mask and regulate her oxygen. She felt a tug on her tanks and turned to see that Omar was checking her harness.

"Thanks," she said.

He nodded. "I will be at your back," he said softly. "I hope there's no need for me to be there, but I will be watching you." He took the heavy light from her. Each pair would share one light. "I'll carry this."

"I've worked with John on two other expeditions. He's always like this, but he is excellent at reconstructing sites."

Omar nodded, then adjusted his own mask. Through the plastic shield, his dark eyes searched hers. Beth turned away and felt his gaze scan down her body, sending tiny little prickles of awareness all through her.

She went to the side of the boat and dropped backward into the water.

Almost immediately she felt a concussion in the water beside her and a swirl of bubbles as Omar dropped in beside her. The site of the sunken city had already been marked by other scientists, and they followed the markers down through the depths.

Beth's first glimpse of Herakleion made her stop her progress and simply stare. In all her excursions to date, she'd always worked to bring a buried site from the soil, carefully brushing layer after layer of soil away from the ruins. In this instance, the city rested on the white-sand floor of the sea. Some silt had built up, but most of the city was visible, rising from the floor of the sea like Atlantis.

Entire buildings were still intact. Beth's crew stopped behind her, all of them staring at what had once been a thriving seaport.

Beth motioned her crew forward and they swam into the city, the three pairs each covering a different quadrant as they searched for an edifice that might be a temple to the goddess Con.

True to his word, Omar stayed just behind her. She found his presence both a comfort and a distraction as she swam through the watery streets.

The scientists who'd done the initial work on the city had determined that an earthquake on the coast of Egypt had sent Herakleion and Menouthis into the sea.

She saw that several ornate buildings, which had once been supported by columns, had collapsed. All the columns had fallen in the same direction, indicating that it was indeed an earthquake.

Omar touched her shoulder, pointing to the columns, and she was again struck by his knowledge of her profession. She swam on, wondering about the mysterious Omar Dukhan. Why was he working as her guide?

There was far more to the man than he'd presented when he'd applied to lead her expedition. Far more.

She found that she was troubled by that thought as she led the way down a narrow alley. A slight movement up ahead made her halt. Small schools of fish swam by, monochromatic flashes of silver in the dark water. Near the surface, she knew, they would take on the iridescent hues of blue, yellow, red and green.

When Omar touched her shoulder, she pointed ahead to where a swirl of water sent fish darting and weaving away.

Omar kept a hand on her shoulder until he slipped past her, turning on a diving light whose beam cut through the water and revealed a narrow alley.

Almost at its end a huge black shape spun, whirling sand and fish in all directions. Omar reached back and caught Beth's hand, pulling her forward.

Her first instinct was to resist, but Omar's gentle tug brought her alongside him as he moved slowly toward the black shape, the light beam shifting from side to side until the giant ray was fully revealed.

The black wings of the creature seemed to cover the entire alley as it spun and lifted into the water above them, a dark shadow passing swiftly over their heads.

Beth had done extensive diving, but she'd never seen a ray that big. They both watched as the creature disappeared.

This time Omar led the way into the alley.

While the other divers had selected the heart of the city to begin their search, Beth was operating on a hunch. Con was a goddess who came and went in Herakleion. Alexandria was actually the place she'd called home, as had her ancestors. Because much of Con's fortune-telling abilities came in dreams, Beth was working on the premise that Con's temple might be on the western edge of the city, where the sun set.

Legend had it that one of Con's ancestors was the lover of Alexander the Great, and that she'd waited for his return in the city that bore his name. It was said that this ancient seer was the woman who'd given Alexander his greatest battle strategies. With her ability to see into the future, she could divine the plans of his enemies. Once Alexander knew their plans, he deployed his armies to defeat them.

Most scientists didn't believe in Con or in any of the legends attached to her lineage. But most scientists were men, Beth thought as she swam behind Omar, watching his long legs kick rhythmically.

Men never wanted to believe that women had that kind of power. Or, at least, most men. A question that interested Beth personally was why, if Con had indeed had the power of second sight, she didn't use the power for her own advantage. Why had Con and her female ancestors used their talents for men?

Beth gazed at the doorways of what once must have been a thriving area of the city. Most were hollow openings, the doors either long gone or nonexistent. She was about to follow Omar to a turn in the alley when she saw an engraving on a stout bronze door that was slightly ajar. She stopped to examine it. The long neck, the elegant head of a feline caught her immediate attention. It was a beautifully crafted carving. She traced the pattern with her fingertip. At her slightest touch the door fell open, and she found herself in a narrow entrance hall that led only to darkness.

She felt movement in the water behind her and turned to find that Omar had come back for her. She pointed into the hallway, and he fumbled with the light, finally bringing the beam to illuminate the interior.

Just as she was about to swim forward, Omar dropped the light. It seemed to fall in slow motion, as if it would never strike the bottom. Omar followed it, but he was too slow. The light struck the floor of the sea and went out.

Left in darkness, Beth wanted to cry or curse. She was on the right track—the proof that she so desperately needed had been within her grasp. But without the light, it would be insane to go into the dark recesses of the building. Most sea creatures were completely harmless, but not all of them.

Omar tapped her shoulder and made apologetic gestures. She forced herself to pantomime that she understood. It was an accident.

Checking her watch, she made a decision. She would send Omar back to the boat for another light. She would mark this spot with some of the floating markers she'd brought along and then try to find some other members of her crew and use *their* light.

She tried to make her decision clear to Omar, regretting each moment that she hadn't purchased the more expensive dive equipment that would have allowed verbal communication. Hindsight was always twenty-twenty. She'd scrimped on the dive suits to be able to buy the underwater video, still-camera equipment and optic computer that would document her find.

Finally giving up on making Omar understand, she marked the spot with a balloon that she tied to the doorway and began to go in search of other crew members.

Omar swam behind her, keeping close enough to stay constantly in her thoughts. He was a highly perceptive man, and one who knew about diving. Why had it been so difficult to make him understand her need for another light? She gnawed at that question as she swam.

They'd swum for ten minutes when Omar tapped her shoulder, indicating that he was headed up for another light. Beth nodded, then continued on her way to find John and Ray or Judy and Sam.

She'd memorized the quadrants of the city that the others were searching and swam toward the nearest section with as much speed as she could muster. She saw the air bubbles before she saw the divers. John Gilmore was examining what could only be a sarcophagus. Camera at his eye, he was documenting the carvings and hieroglyphics that covered the stone funery.

He must have sensed her arrival because he looked up, lowering the camera. Ray swam over from the carvings he'd been studying. Beth motioned to them to help find the others. They immediately swam north while she headed west. It didn't take her long to find Sam and Judy. She led Sam and Judy back to where she'd discovered John and Ray.

As soon as John and Ray returned, Beth made a few motions, describing her discovery, and they all swam back toward the alley.

Eyes open for the floating marker, Beth covered the same territory twice before she realized that, somehow, the marker was gone.

Borrowing John's light, she searched the area until she found the alley. Once there, she led her crew to the doorway with the carved cat. Watching John's face, she knew that her intuition was right on. His face registered the same excitement she felt, and he was already preparing the video camera.

Slowly, in the beam of two lights, the small crew entered the dark hallway, swimming carefully until they were suddenly in an open room that brought all of them to a stop.

"Holy Christmas," Beth mouthed around her regulator as she stared at the incredible statues that lined two sides of the chamber. This place had to be a temple.

John pointed to a limestone altar at the front of the room. Behind it stood another statue—that of an incredibly beautiful woman. In the center of her forehead was a third eye.

"Con," Beth mouthed.

"Con," John said, removing his mouthpiece and mouthing the word so that air bubbles burst from his mouth and sped toward the surface.

"We've found her," Beth said, even though she knew no one could possibly understand what she was saying.

OMAR HUNG BACK, the light in his hand, as he watched the divers enter the alley. Even though he'd gone back and cut the balloon marker free, Beth had been able to find the alley with little trouble. Now they were undoubtedly in the temple of Con.

Omar had never seen the temple, but he was aware that it existed. Until the scientists had found Herakleion on the bottom of the sea, the secret of Con's temple had seemed safe for eternity.

Now, though, the trail to the lost City of Con was at stake. And Omar's sacred vow was in danger of being broken.

He waited until the last of the research crew had disappeared in the watery temple before he swam down to join them. Whatever he did, he could not let Beth or any of the crew members suspect he was trying to hamper their efforts.

Slipping through the dark hallway, he stopped at the entrance to the temple sanctuary. For centuries this temple had been buried safely beneath the sea. He knew all about it from the stories that had been handed down to him through the ages. He knew that Beth had made an important discovery in her quest.

He swam slowly to the front of the chamber, stopping at the altar to look up into the face of a statue that could easily have been modeled after his mother. Con. The goddess who had unlocked the secrets of the third eye, the woman to whom he could directly trace his blood.

He stared at the statue, comparing it to the ones in the secret city. Very slowly he drifted to the statue and touched the cheek of the goddess. He'd never doubted the legends of his people, but now he had looked upon the goddess and her temple. He would have much to tell his followers when he returned to the desert.

Several of the scientists had gathered along one wall. He watched them, suddenly aware that Beth wasn't in their number. He turned, searching the darkened chamber until he found her suspended in the water and staring at him.

He swallowed. Beth was perceptive. He'd given himself away by the way he touched the statue. For a second he thought of going to her, but then he swam over to see what had caught the interest of the other scientists.

The hieroglyphics on the wall were beautifully wrought, and Omar felt a stab of worry. They could easily be directions to the City of Con. He watched as John Gilmore began the process of filming the entire wall. John moved slowly over the symbols, giving the camera plenty of time to record. Carefully he began to work his way around the temple.

The other scientists fanned out, each one working on a statue or some aspect of the temple. Omar knew they had to work fast. They had only so much oxygen left in their tanks. Against all odds, Beth had come to Herakleion and discovered the secret that had been buried in the watery grave for more than two thousand years.

Omar knew that he was going to have to figure out a way to re-bury that secret, if he intended to keep his lost city safe from the prying eyes of the world.

Okay, Miss Explorer has been down there long enough. Omar has been back for another light, but I haven't seen hide nor hair of the lady scientist. I'm beginning to get a little nervous.

Now my sassy, red-haired friend, Mauve, is squealing with delight. She's got a death grip on one of those machines, and she's jumping up and down with excitement. The skipper is looking at her like she's crazy.

I think it's safe to assume that Beth has hit pay dirt. She must have found the temple she was looking for. I'm delighted for her. Now maybe we can get off this creaking, lurching boat and get back to dry land.

Someone is transmitting images from the bottom to the equipment Mauve is operating. Now I can just slip up here and see what all the excitement is about. At first glance it looks like that old Lloyd Bridges show, Seahunt. *Lots of watery images and… What's that white thing? Looks like a woman.*

A woman with an eye smack in the middle of her forehead.

Con.

So Beth has found her. This is exciting. Now here comes a bunch of images of what looks like drawings intended to say something. I'm no Egyptologist, but I'd call those things hieroglyphics. Someone is going to have a lot of fun trying to figure out what they say.

Hmm, there's the image of Con with a white crown holding a handful of some wheatlike grain. And it would seem it's Con again, but this time her crown is red. And she's riding a bull. I don't have a clue what it means, but I like a woman who can ride bulls.

It must have taken whoever carved these things in

stone half a lifetime to do it. They're very complex. I just wonder if anyone can really decipher what they mean.

I remember what Beth said earlier about doubt. She's right. Doubt is the thing that can kill genius. Beth will eventually decipher the hieroglyphics, and when she does, we're on our way into the desert.

We have two days for her to work on this. Now we'll see exactly how good John Gilmore is at his work.

Look, the camera is on Omar. He's staring at the hieroglyphics as if he could burn them into his memory—or else burn them off the stone wall. There's something about our desert guide that bears watching. Close watching. And I'm just the cat for the job.

Chapter Five

Beth could barely force herself to sit still as the boat sped back to Alexandria. She'd planned on at least three days of diving. It was almost unimaginable that she'd found the temple on the first day of the underwater excursion. This put her two days ahead on the expedition. It was almost as if Con were guiding her.

She smiled at that thought. She'd had so much doubt about this adventure. All her professional life she'd been content to settle in to work the sites that others had found. Her work was important, but it was always the work of the follower, the detail work that made for footnotes in history. The lost City of Con was a major discovery. She would make her mark as a leader, as a woman with a vision of the past. More than that, though, she would change the way history viewed women.

Sure, Cleopatra had been viewed as a powerful ruler, but it was her romantic interludes for which she was famous. On the other hand, Con and her progeny had been the guiding force behind the Ptolemy rule. She had served as the eye to the future for the leaders of Egypt, as well as for many of the rest of the world.

What if there were actual records of Con's predictions? Or the predictions of her female ancestors and descendants? What if there was some description of how these women were able to predict the future?

Beth felt chill bumps shift over her body at the very thought. Modern science was just beginning to accept the power of the mind. What if there was written documentation of that power and how it might be accessed?

The possibility of what that could mean to the world made Beth short of breath. She stood up and began to pace the deck of the boat.

"How long do you think it will take you to decipher the hieroglyphics?" Omar asked her.

She'd failed to see him approach, and his question caught her off guard. She turned to him and was aware of the sun's light rippling through his dark hair, the glint of his tanned chest. Unlike the other men, whose pale skins had begun to redden, he was a creature of the sun.

"I don't know. Just looking at them, it seems to be a combination of symbolic pictures and symbols that also represent sound. It looks pretty complex."

"I wonder why they chose to use symbols," Omar said. "They could have written it."

She nodded. "Yes, the Egyptians were using a written alphabet at the time."

"Perhaps the hieroglyphics were used deliberately."

"To prevent outsiders from finding the city?" Beth asked. This seemed to be a theme with Omar.

"'Outsiders' is a harsh term. I do know that the followers of Con were a very secretive bunch." He smiled to take the sting out of his words. "I think that for them, everyone who wasn't absolutely bound to the group was considered an outsider."

"They lived a long time ago. Perhaps they'll look kindly on another woman who simply wants to understand them."

He stared deeply into her eyes. "Is that really what you want, Beth?"

It was the first time he'd used her name, and she knew that his question was loaded with meaning. "It's my job, Omar. It's what I do because I love doing it. I think by learning about the past, we can prevent mistakes now. We can learn from those who came before us."

"And is all this learning for yourself or for the glory that will come with it?"

She hesitated. "I would be lying if I didn't say both. I want to be recognized and acknowledged as a top professional in my field, but I could have gone in search of any number of other sites of archaeological importance."

"So what is it about the City of Con that drew you to it?"

"It's not the city. It's Con." Beth wondered if a man could ever understand her motives. She suddenly decided to try to make Omar see. "I dream about her," she said softly. "I see her, and I want to know what role she played in history. I want her to have the credit she deserves."

"Perhaps she didn't want credit."

Beth smiled. "I can't know for certain, but neither can you."

Omar leaned closer, sending a shudder of pleasure through Beth as his whisper lightly touched her ear. "What if I told you that I, too, dream of Con? And in my dreams, she tells me that the past is best left shrouded in mystery."

His words left Beth with a sensation of dizziness. It was almost as if he spoke straight to her heart. The blood rushed through her veins, and she felt her body tremble. His hand caught her elbow, a strong grip that steadied her.

"I'm sorry," she mumbled, horrified that she'd come very close to falling. "I don't know what came over me."

"You haven't eaten anything today except a roll," he reminded her, gently leading her to a seat. "There are sandwiches in one of those baskets. I'll get one for you."

He was back at her side in moments with a chicken sandwich and a cold bottle of water. Beth took the water gratefully. Her throat was parched, and she couldn't remember the last time she'd had a drink of anything as cold and delicious as the water.

"Are you okay?" he asked when she'd finished drinking.

She nodded without meeting his eyes. "Yes, perfectly. I really can't think what happened. I've never felt anything like that before." Her cheeks reddened at the memory. He'd whispered in her ear and she'd almost dropped to the floor. It was humiliating. "I'm not some delicate flower, you know."

"We'll continue our discussion after you've eaten

and rested,'' Omar said. "Perhaps you would have dinner with me tonight?''

Caught off guard yet again, Beth was about to say no when Mauve came and sat down beside her. "Was that a dinner invitation?'' she asked.

"Yes. I'd like to show Beth some of the city. Places she can't see without a knowledgeable guide.''

"She'd love to have dinner,'' Mauve said.

"Mauve!'' Beth finally found her tongue.

"Oh, for heaven's sake,'' Mauve said, frowning. "You'd be a fool to turn down a real tour of Alexandria. Just do it and remember some of the places, so you can take me when you're a famous anthropologist.''

"I'll be in the hotel lobby at seven o'clock,'' Omar said. He smiled his thanks to Mauve. "You won't be disappointed in Alexandria. She is a city with many, many secrets and a nature that applauds the sensual.''

He walked away, leaving the two women sitting together.

"You had no right to accept a dinner invitation for me,'' Beth said.

"Hold it right there, Beth. The man is the best-looking example of male flesh I've seen in years. He wants to show you his city, which is something any scientist would find fascinating. He has good manners. Why wouldn't you go?''

"We have a working relationship. I don't know that it's a good idea to combine work and pleasure.''

"Ah, so you do admit he is a pleasure. This, at least, is progress. I was beginning to fear that you had forgotten what a good-looking man can do for a woman.''

"He is handsome." Beth's skin tingled as she said the words. The memory of his whisper slipped across her flesh.

"And mysterious and intriguing and compelling, and just about illegally sexy." Mauve sighed. "I wonder if he has relatives."

"I'll be sure to ask," Beth said.

"You do that. And make arrangements for them to be on the overland portion of the trip. By the way, I'm going to start working on the hieroglyphics tonight. I mean, if you're going to party all the time, someone has to work."

Beth tugged a lock of her friend's long, red hair. "You're not very good at playing the role of martyr, Mauve. I'd give it up and concentrate more on being the troublemaker. That's where you excel."

"Thank you, darling," Mauve drawled. "I do try. I think I also show tremendous potential as a match-maker. Just keep in mind I expect a percentage of the dowry."

Beth laughed out loud. "If Omar is thinking I have a dowry, he's going to be very disappointed."

Mauve put a finger to her lips. "Shush! I've already misled him in that direction."

"How?" Beth asked. Mauve was incorrigible, but she was always entertaining.

"When he was asking about the funding for the trip, I didn't exactly say that you came from a wealthy family, but I did sort of imply that."

Beth felt a tiny chill in the region of her heart. "He was asking about the funding?"

"I gather you didn't pay him for his services up

front. I suppose he was just making sure you were good for the cash.''

"What did he say?" Beth used her paper napkin to wipe her already clean hands.

"Why? What's wrong?"

"Nothing. I just wonder why he didn't ask me."

"Because he's sweet on you," Mauve said. "Wages aren't exactly the topic you want to talk about with someone you want to go out with, especially not if what you're asking is basically whether that person really has the money to afford you."

"And what did you tell him?" Beth tried not to show how disturbing she found Omar's question.

"That you were flush with money. That you had the blessing of a major backer, and that your family was behind you a hundred percent. I thought it would look better if it was a professional trip, and I assured him that you had a solid backer who'd put money in the bank account. But I also led him to believe that you had your own resources, if necessary."

"Great," Beth said, forcing her voice to sound light and her mouth to smile. "Now if it turns out that our desert guide wants an American hostage to hold for ransom, he'll believe someone in my family can pay for me."

"Oh, if he's going to hold you hostage, I don't think it'll be for ransom." Mauve stood up. "John's over there fooling with my equipment. Let me make sure he doesn't do something stupid and lose those images I captured."

"I want a printout as soon as possible," Beth said.

"You're wish is my command." Mauve did a low

bow that made Beth groan. "I'll expect a full report on your evening," Mauve murmured as she backed up and away.

OMAR WATCHED the exchange between the two women with some trepidation. He'd asked Mauve about the backing for the expedition as soon as he'd seen all the equipment. Beth had brought some of the finest in high-tech gear, and it had cost a pretty penny. The video images that John had captured in the temple had been brought back, fed into a computer, and Mauve would soon be able to print them out in detail. It was the most exact process for studying underwater finds available.

In questioning Mauve, though, he'd revealed his interest in Beth's business. He'd tried to couch his questions so that it appeared he was only interested in making sure his salary would be paid. Mauve had believed him, but he wasn't certain Beth would.

He glanced at her and felt a disturbing reaction in his groin. There was something about Beth Bradshaw that made his desire burn hot. His gaze lingered on her slender neck, the cleavage revealed by the scoop neck of her simple swimsuit. She was a woman with all the sweetness that implied. And she was so much more.

Any man would be physically drawn to her, but Omar found that as much as he wanted to touch her smooth skin, he was equally drawn to the sparkle in her dark eyes, the intensity of her passion when she spoke of Con. She believed in Con, and her passion was one he shared for the woman who had shaped the history of his country and the ancient world.

Omar had known many women, some of them so-phisticates of the city, others the sensuous women of the desert. A few knew the secrets of Con, but none cared the way Beth Bradshaw did.

The problem was, Beth had come to Egypt to reveal Con to the world. Omar, as the leading descendant of Con, had taken a vow to keep the location of the lost city a secret. His thoughts turned to his brother, Harad. As the older sibling, Harad rightfully should have taken over the desert stronghold of Con. He had been raised in the ways of the desert, taught to revere the sacred-ness of the lost city and what it meant to the three hundred members of his tribe.

Harad, though, had forsaken the desert and his her-itage.

Both brothers had been educated in the finest uni-versities, taught professions where they could excel and achieve. Their mother, Aleta, had been wise enough to know that their world was rapidly changing. She wanted her sons to be able to make the transition from desert tribesmen to successful businessmen, should it become necessary.

Harad had seen the wisdom of that decision when Aleta died. Angered by the way she'd refused to leave the lost city to get medical attention for her heart con-dition, he'd buried his mother and left the desert for-ever. Stepping into the breach, Omar had taken up the leadership of his people. And so it had been for the past five years.

In that time he'd been able to live the desert life of his people without interference. Beth Bradshaw now threatened that life.

No matter his personal feelings toward her, Omar knew that he would have to stop her from finding the lost city.

The boat docked and he helped the others unload the equipment. Beth was busy, and he watched with pleasure the way she led her crew. She was not a dictator, but someone who led by example.

At her side was the strange black cat. Familiar. As he hefted a heavy piece of equipment and loaded it onto the dolly, Omar studied the animal. The cat was unusual, even in a country with many evolved cats. And he'd obviously appointed himself as Beth's guardian.

But where had an American cat come from—if indeed a high five indicated such citizenship? How had Familiar ended up in Alexandria? That, perhaps, was a mystery that would never be resolved.

The sun was setting as Omar helped carry the last of the equipment into the hotel. Some had gone to Beth's room, but the pieces he was interested in were put in Mauve's room. She was going to take the stored images and duplicate them so that the entire crew could begin work on deciphering the message. It was Mauve's room where he needed to pay his next nocturnal visit.

He retrieved his own diving equipment and was walking across the lobby when he heard his name called.

"Still hanging around?" John Gilmore asked.

Omar turned to face him. "My work has just concluded."

"What is it you really want?" John asked.

Omar felt his gut tighten. John had been merely an annoyance, but his habit of calling attention to him was becoming dangerous. "I want to do my job," Omar said softly.

"And that would be what, exactly?"

"It should be obvious, even to you." Omar did not want an argument, but he wasn't about to back down from the arrogant scientist.

"Beth seems to be more in your line of interest than a job," John accused.

"You're jealous?" Omar asked, surprised. "Do you have an interest in Ms. Bradshaw?"

"An interest in making sure she's not hurt."

"Why would I want to hurt her?" Omar asked. He was angry at John's accusations, but he was also amused. He'd never suspected that the prickly scientist had a romantic interest in Beth.

"That's exactly what I intend to find out. I don't know who or what you are, but you're not some simple desert guide."

Omar's jaw clenched. "Nothing in my country is simple. To survive the desert requires great skill and knowledge. You should remember that, Mr. Gilmore. Now I have business to attend to."

"I'm going to check you out, Dukhan. You can count on it."

Omar walked out of the lobby, his diving gear in one hand. John Gilmore could check all he wanted. Omar had gone to great lengths to create his biography. It would take someone a lot smarter than John Gilmore to discover the truth.

BETH STUDIED her reflection in the mirror. The sheath dress she'd chosen was a vivid swirl of bright colors

that offset her dark hair and tanned skin. The hemline
was high, showing off her legs, and she wondered what
Omar Dukhan's reaction would be. In Alexandria she'd
seen everything from the tribal dress of robes and the
traditional covered head to teenage punk. As a man of
the desert, would Omar expect a more conservative
dinner date? Too bad.

The phone by her bed rang, and she moved to pick
up the receiver.

"Ms. Bradshaw, how was your first day of diving?"

She instantly recognized the cultured voice of Nazar
Bettina, the man who was backing her expedition.

"Mr. Be—"

"Please, Ms. Bradshaw, do not use my name. The
phone lines are never safe."

Beth's intake of breath was sharp.

"I don't mean to frighten you," Nazar said softly.
"It is just that I don't want my name linked with this
expedition until the success is assured. In my position,
public failure at anything is never a good thing."

Beth relaxed a little. Nazar Bettina had been very
specific about the fact that his backing must not be
revealed until he gave the word. "I'm sorry," she said.
"I wasn't thinking."

His chuckle was soft, velvety, and she wondered
what he looked like. Nazar Bettina was a man who'd
calmly put half a million dollars on the line and never
even met her face-to-face.

"So, tell me, how was the dive? Did you find anything interesting?"

"We found the temple," Beth said, her excitement

bubbling over in her voice. "It was incredible. I went straight to it, as if I were being guided by some unseen force."

"Perhaps the goddess Con has found a new devotee. In the older legends, it is said she had the capability to slip into the dreams of others."

"Do you suppose we'll find some documentation of those abilities?" Beth asked.

"If you do, you'll become a very wealthy woman, as well as a famous one. And I will be hailed as a very wise man for backing you."

"Are you in the city?" Beth asked, suddenly wanting to show her benefactor the hieroglyphics.

"No, my dear, I'm far, far away. I did want to caution you, Beth. Your undertaking can excite tremendous jealousy. I know you're wise enough to keep the details of your work to yourself. I call only to emphasize that point."

Again Beth felt a tightening of the skin at the base of her neck. "I'm perfectly safe," she assured him. "I have a wonderful guide, and we're going to set off for the desert as soon as we decipher the directions."

"Directions to the lost city?" Nazar asked, excitement creeping into his own voice.

"I believe that's what we discovered."

"Excellent! You have far exceeded my expectations. Now I must go. Business awaits me." He chuckled again. "I must keep my accounts rich, in case you require more money for this adventure."

"You've been quite generous—"

"And you've been quite successful. I want you to

know that if you learn the way to the lost city, whatever you need to get there will be provided."

"We have everything we need," Beth assured him.

"Goodbye, my dear. I'll be watching over you."

The phone line went dead and Beth hung up just as a knock came on her door. She opened it to find Omar standing there. His traditional robes were gone. Instead, he wore slacks and a cotton shirt of fine, pale ivory. Beth had never seen a more handsome man.

He stepped back to look her over from head to toe. "A transformation," he said, smiling. "From scientist to ravishing beauty. I do believe you must have learned the secrets of Con."

Beth had never been one to be taken in by flattery, but his words warmed her. "I could say the same about you. Desert guide to *GQ* model."

"I'm hungry," Omar said, holding out his arm. "I've planned a special evening for you. One I hope you'll never forget."

As Beth began to shut her door, she saw the black cat dart out into the hallway. He must have come in through the balcony window, because she hadn't seen him since she'd unloaded the equipment from the boat. In fact, he came and went at will via the balcony.

She'd never had a date with a desert guide and a black-cat shadow. Beth took a deep breath. She would have so many wonderful adventures to tell Amelia— when she finally got a chance to talk to her "sister." She made a mental note to call the Corbets first thing in the morning. Before she set out for the desert, she wanted to be sure to let her adopted family know where she was and that she was on her way to the top of her profession.

Chapter Six

Omar poured the red wine into Beth's glass. The longer the evening went on, the more he had to force himself to pretend enjoyment. His conscience had quit nibbling and begun gnawing on him.

"You know Alexandria well," Beth said. "I've seen parts of the city I never dreamed existed." She looked around the small club that was a combination of exotic Middle Eastern culture and Manhattan café. The stucco walls were covered with colorful mosaics, and palms swayed gently in the breeze of ceiling fans. In the background a combo played softly. "So how is it that a man of the desert knows this city like it was his childhood home? Tell me about yourself."

Her cheeks were flushed from dancing and the wine, and Omar wanted nothing more than to lean across the table and kiss her lips. But as leader of his people, his desires came secondary. No matter how much he wanted to forget that, he could not allow himself the luxury.

"I was born in the desert," he said. "My mother was part of a small nomadic tribe. She saw the changes coming to our people, though, and sent me to Paris for an education.''

"And you came back to the desert. Why?'' Beth sipped her wine.

Duty would be the simplest way to explain his choices, but it was also insufficient. "The life of a nomad is a life of freedom,'' he said, choosing his words carefully. "I had a role to play there that wasn't available in Alexandria or Paris or Belgium. There are many things I love about it.''

Beth was searching his face, looking for the truth behind his words. She was a perceptive woman, and he was struck once again by the thought of how much his mother would have enjoyed her.

"Are your parents still alive?'' Beth asked as if she could read his mind.

"No. My father left us when I was very young. My mother died five years ago.''

"At least you had your mother for a long time.''

"Yes,'' he said. "But you didn't.'' He could see it in her eyes.

"No, my folks were killed when I was ten. Sometimes it seems like an eternity since it happened, and sometimes it seems like it happened only yesterday.''

"I know.'' He drained his own glass and refilled it, pouring more into hers. His plans required her to be drunk. But he was the one feeling the effects—of her beauty and her love of life.

"I had a best friend in school. Amelia Corbet. Her family practically adopted me. If it hadn't been for them, I don't really know what would have happened to me. They put me through school and…they're my family now.''

''They must be good people.''

''The best.'' Beth spoke with emotion. ''Amelia is the exact opposite of me, but we're like sisters.''

Beth's smile was wobbly, and Omar knew his plan was working. It was just a matter of time now.

''By the way, Mauve misled you,'' Beth said.

Omar was instantly alert. ''About what?''

''The Corbets do have money, but I don't. There's no one to ransom me if I'm taken by desert pirates.'' She laughed. ''I'm afraid it would be more like 'The Ransom of Red Chief.' They'd probably pay you money to take me back.''

''Somehow I doubt that,'' Omar said. His tone was light, but his feelings for Beth were growing by the moment. He would have to ask the goddess why the woman who'd been sent to destroy his heritage had to be so desirable. He wasn't a man whose head was turned by a pretty face. Beth was more than pretty, though. She had a true heart.

''I do want to reassure you that I have money in the bank to pay you,'' Beth continued.

''I didn't doubt your word,'' he said carefully. ''Mauve assured me that you have a very generous backer.''

He saw her face change, a mask of caution dropping over her features. ''Yes. I'm fortunate.''

''Would it be improper to ask who this backer is?''

Beth stared directly into his eyes as she took a breath. ''Normally, no. In this particular situation, my backer has requested total anonymity until the expedition is completed.''

"Ah, a man who has a high profile and doesn't want to be associated with a failure?" Omar was guessing, but he saw that he'd hit his mark.

Beth shrugged. "You could say that, I suppose. Whatever his reasons, I intend to honor his request." She licked her bottom lip. "I honor my word whenever I give it."

"A quality that is beyond measure," Omar said, steering the conversation in another direction. He'd learned as much as he was going to learn about who was backing the expedition. She'd told him far more than she knew.

"Are you a man of honor?" Beth asked.

Omar was glad that the candlelit table and his dark complexion hid the flush that warmed his cheeks. "Honor is a difficult thing to judge," he said carefully.

"That sounds like a dodge." Beth put her hand across the table to touch his. "You strike me as a man who holds honor in high esteem."

"I do," he said, knowing that she would never judge his actions honorable. "Honor *is* a difficult thing to judge, Beth," he repeated. "Perhaps that's why many religions stress the importance of not judging others."

"I used to believe that there are only right and wrong answers or decisions or actions." Beth's gaze dropped to her plate. "I'm not so sure anymore."

Omar could no longer resist. He turned his hand to take hold of hers, using his thumb to tease her palm. "You're a wise woman, Beth. I don't know if you'll ever find the City of Con, but I believe that the goddess would be proud to have you there.''

Beth looked up, her eyes shimmering in the candlelight. ''Thank you, Omar. I can't tell you what that means to me.''

He stood up, unable to continue the charade of the evening any longer. If he had to betray Beth's trust, he didn't have to do it with candlelight and wine. She didn't deserve to be tricked by the snake and then bitten while she clutched him to her bosom.

Beth stood up, too, uncertainty in her eyes. ''What's wrong?'' she asked.

''It's late. We should go.''

Beth stepped toward him, her hand reaching for his face. ''Omar? What is it?''

From beneath the table, the strange black cat darted, twining into her legs and causing her to stumble. Omar caught her just in time, pulling her into his arms.

Beth looked up at him, her lips open in invitation. It was more than he could stand. He kissed her, and in that moment he knew that he was lost.

He'd intended to keep her out late until he had to carry her to bed. He'd wanted only an opportunity to search through her things.

Now he had other plans. Without saying a word he led her outside and into a cab, where she held his hand in a tight grip on the short ride to the Palace Hotel, the finest European-style hotel in the city. At the desk he whispered his brother's name, and a key was slipped into his hand.

With his arm around Beth, he led her into an elevator. They rode to the top floor in silence. Omar inserted the key and the elevator door opened on the penthouse.

"This is yours?" Beth asked in wonder, stepping off the elevator and into a room that had been furnished with flowing curtains and pillows on beautiful carpets.

"No. I have no desire to live in the city. But I have friends who do," Omar said.

"Wealthy friends," Beth added. She turned to face him. "Why did you bring me here?"

He could see that she knew but wanted to hear him say it. "I intend to make love to you," he said, shrugging out of his jacket as he spoke.

Beth swallowed, but she didn't back away as he approached. He wrapped his arms around her and pulled her into an embrace. When his lips found hers, she responded without hesitation.

It took only seconds for the kiss to flame through his blood, and his hands began to unzip her dress.

Omar knew that he was making a mistake. A tragic mistake. Beth Bradshaw was a woman he would have to betray before the month was out. To protect his people and his heritage, he would have to lie to Beth and deceive her. Her plans and dreams would be crushed because of him, and she would be labeled a failure and ridiculed by her colleagues, even though she was one hundred percent right in her theories. All of this, and he would be the tool of her destruction.

Yet he couldn't resist her. He had to have her, to touch her silky skin and feel her thick brown hair brush over his face. Never in his life had a physical desire demanded such gratification. He would have Beth and pay the consequences later. There were times when the devil be damned.

BETH FELT AS IF someone else had crawled into her skin. Some wanton woman who was ruled by physical cravings. It was utterly insane to let Omar Dukhan touch her this way. But his hand glided over her breast, and even through the material of her dress she felt her body respond. It was madness, but such sweet madness that she couldn't bring herself to stop him.

She'd walked into the hotel, stepped into the elevator and walked into this apartment, the whole time knowing where things were headed. At any moment she could have stopped. Yet she felt powerless to do so. While her logical mind argued for her to zip her dress back up and leave, her body demanded more of his touch, her lips sought his burning kiss.

She felt her dress slide from her shoulders and fall to the floor. Her fingers were at the buttons of his shirt, working fast to reveal the hard muscles of his chest and stomach. He was the most magnificent man she'd ever seen. He moved her in a way that she'd never experienced. Whatever the price—and there would be one—she would pay it.

He led her to a bed of pillows on the floor, and she sank onto them, pulling him with her. The moon shone through a big window, gilding in silver the hanging draperies that surrounded the bed.

Omar lifted himself on his arms so that he could look down at her. "I've never wanted a woman the way I want you," he said.

"Don't talk," she whispered, reaching up to touch his face and finally to pull him down on top of her.

BETH AWOKE as dawn was touching the sky with pink. The draperies that hung around her were blushing with the first hint of color, and it took her a moment to remember where she was. What she had done came flooding back, a tidal wave of sensations and emotions.

The pillows beside her were empty, and when she sat up, she could find no sign of Omar.

Beth stood up, her body feeling strange and alien. In the long hours of the night, she'd experienced sensations and explosive emotions that she'd never known existed. Omar had possessed her body in a way that made it his own—and had given her the most exquisite pleasure.

And now he was gone.

She scrambled into her clothes, wondering where she was. She'd paid no attention to direction the night before and had no idea what part of Alexandria the hotel was in. She only knew that she wanted to get back to her hotel before the rest of her crew woke up and began looking for her.

It was highly unprofessional to carry on with a member of the crew. In her entire career, she'd never allowed herself to date a co-worker, much less sleep with one. She'd broken her own rules, and now she'd woken up to find herself abandoned in a hotel room. A penthouse, yes, but still a hotel room.

As she tried to comb some order into her hair with her fingers, she knew there was only one solution to what had happened. Omar could not possibly guide the crew into the desert. She would have to find another guide—preferably one who was old, ugly and married.

She felt a thud of horror in her chest. Omar had never said he wasn't married. What if he was? What if the reason he'd left her was so he could return to his wife?

That thought was more than she could stand. She found her purse and was ready to bolt out of the hotel. The knock that came at the door almost made her scream. It took all her resolve to calmly open it.

A room-service cart stood outside the door, but there was no attendant. There was only a single red rose with a note attached.

Hands trembling, Beth opened the note.

"Last night was the most incredible night I've ever spent with anyone. I've gone to check the final arrangements for the trip. Although I can't share breakfast with you, I ask that you reserve lunch for me. I will have all the details of the trip ready to present to you then. Omar."

She put the note down and pushed the cart into the penthouse. Opening the lids of the serving dishes, she found a traditional American breakfast, from bacon to grits. Grits! Where had Omar found grits in Egypt? He was more than amazing.

Her fears and worries diminished as she sat down and ate. He hadn't abandoned her; he'd simply gone to take care of business. It didn't lessen the fact that she'd stepped over a line by sleeping with a crew member, but it did make her feel better. Much better.

She finished eating and then calmly left the hotel,

hailing a cab and arriving at her hotel just as the pa-
trons began to come down for breakfast.

She saw John and Mauve, arguing as usual, and she
darted behind the stairs as they passed. She didn't want
them to see her. She wasn't ashamed of her actions,
but she didn't want to answer any questions. Particularly from John.

She made it to her room and ran a hot bath. She was
about to step into the tub when the black cat sailed
through the window.

"Me-ow," he said softly.

"Meow to you." She scratched his head. She had a
vague recollection that somehow the cat had precipi-
tated that first kiss between her and Omar. Yes, he'd
tripped her, sending her into Omar's arms. Had it not
been for that moment, she might have ended up back
in her hotel room, alone in her own bed.

"I don't know whether I should kiss you or scold
you," she said, rubbing the cat's head. "Only time will
tell." She kissed his head and was rewarded with a
long, loud purr.

*AH, MISS EXPLORER showers me with kisses and affec-
tion. I think it's a spillover from her evening with Desert Hawk. What am I going to do? I thought if I could
throw them together, Omar would give up whatever
secret plan he's working on. Not so. He left her in the
Palace Hotel and came right over here to go through
her things.*

*I don't know what he's looking for, but he hasn't
stopped. Right now he's out in the gardens, waiting for
some new opportunity to snoop, I'm sure. I guess I'll*

just have to make it my business to be here when he comes back.

I know he's drawn to Miss Explorer. Heck, he's mush in her hands. But he's also pulled in another direction. One look at his face when he's looking at Beth and a half-blind feline could see it. Of course, the humanoids don't see anything. My goodness, they have no real sensitivity at all. How did they multiply in such great numbers?

I look around this city and see the lovely cats lounging and walking the streets and bazaars. Peter is correct. There are too many cats—and too many humans. Peter and Eleanor are doing everything they can to promote responsible population control, and I'm right behind them on all efforts. For cats, dogs and people.

Speaking of Peter and Eleanor, they were a little annoyed with me for abandoning them in the airport. But I think I've made them understand that while they have work to do, so do I. I can't say why I'm so compelled to protect Miss Explorer. Must be that she was orphaned, like me. Whatever it is, I can't let Omar hurt her. Now that I've gotten them together, it's sort of my responsibility to make sure he doesn't do anything to permanently damage her.

I think Omar has to realize that while camels can be nasty, vicious creatures, he hasn't seen anything resembling vicious until he sees moi *in a tizzy.*

Besides, now I'm more curious than ever about what he's up to. I may have to put a tail on him. A nice, curly, black one would certainly improve his appearance. Might help his balance, too. Ha-ha, I fear my humor is wasted on humanoids.

Ah, Beth is bathed and changed and ready to go downstairs. I'll hang out to await the next appearance of Desert Hawk.

OMAR STOOD in the middle of Mauve's room. The computer screen wavered and blipped irregularly, making a high, whining sound that spelled impending disaster.

The images that had been captured on the bottom of the sea were gone. The brain of the computer where they'd been stored was destroyed, in such a way that it could be seen as a fault with the computer. Luckily Mauve had left the computer running while she went down to breakfast.

Omar looked around the room. All of the other equipment was untouched, and nothing gave away that he'd been here. The secrets of Con were safe for now.

He heard something and turned swiftly, his stance ready for attack or defense, whatever was necessary. The black cat stepped in through the balcony door, which Omar had left slightly open.

Golden eyes blinking, the cat surveyed the room. Omar felt the cat's assessing gaze take in the leather gloves he wore, the tool belt around his waist. The dying computer.

Familiar looked at Omar and gave a low, deadly hiss.

"It's for the best," he said to the cat—and to himself. "She had to be stopped. It's better now than later on in the desert when she's spent more money, more time, invested more of herself and her future."

Familiar's only answer was a vicious growl.

He didn't have time to hang around and justify

things to a cat. He had to get back into the hotel lobby and pretend that all was well. Omar stepped out onto the balcony. He slid the door closed and used the special tools he'd brought to jimmy the lock back into place. Then he climbed from Mauve's balcony back to Beth's, which had easier access to and from the ground. Swinging himself over, he jumped down and landed softly.

Just as he regained his balance and was tucking the leather gloves into his robe, he heard a chuckle behind him.

"I wondered what was keeping Beth so late in bed," John Gilmore said as he stepped out from beneath the shadow of the arched doorway that offered access to the hotel lobby.

"I suggest you mind your own business." Omar silently cursed his own carelessness and bad luck. John had only seen him come from Beth's balcony and had jumped to the wrong conclusion. One that spared Omar, but put Beth's reputation further in jeopardy.

"Beth used to be a woman of principles. She had rules once. Sleeping with the hired help was beneath her."

Omar started to brush past John, then felt the scientist's hand grip his shoulder. Slowly Omar turned, dark eyes burning with anger.

"Mr. Gilmore, if you touch me again, I'll respond in a way you won't like."

"I'm terrified," John said, laughing. "Why don't you hit me? That way I could have you fired right this minute and you would be out of my hair."

"You are a fool," Omar said, taking long strides to

put as much distance as possible between himself and the man he loathed.

"You're going to ruin Beth," John called out to him. "Everyone on this expedition knows it. You're going to ruin her professionally and personally. That will be on your head for the rest of your life."

Chapter Seven

John was already gone from the restaurant and Mauve was gathering her purse to leave when Beth paused in the doorway. She'd composed her face and was determined to reveal nothing about the night just past.

Mauve's bright smile gave way to a sly look as she crossed the restaurant and stopped beside her friend.

"So, what canary did you swallow?" Mauve asked. "Don't bother to deny it. You may fool the rest of the crew, but I know you've been bad. Very bad, judging from the guilty look you're trying so hard to hide."

Beth shook her head. It was senseless to lie to Mauve.

"So, how was it?" Mauve's eyes danced with curiosity.

Once again Beth only shook her head.

"That incredible? You're going to make me jealous."

"I need some coffee," Beth managed to say. She had so many different emotions. The night with Omar had changed her in some profound way. She wasn't sure what, but she felt the change deep inside.

"While you were out indulging in incredible sex and

misbehavior, I was a very busy woman," Mauve said. "I worked through most of the night."

Beth felt a surge of gratitude. "I should have been here to help."

Mauve only laughed. "I doubt that! You were doing exactly what you should have been doing. Beth, give it a rest. You need something in your life other than a job. I'll tell you the truth. If Omar Dukhan had crooked his little finger at me, I would have abandoned my work, my career, everything. You're a lucky woman, so don't screw it up by playing slave to your job, okay?"

Beth's smile was slow in coming and tentative. "Okay."

"Get some coffee and hurry up to my room. You're not going to believe what I found."

Beth signaled the waiter and asked for a large thermos of coffee and two cups on a tray. The simplest thing would be to take the coffee to Mauve's room where they could go over her findings. Beth felt a tingle of excitement course through her body. Since her arrival in Egypt, her entire life had changed. She was on track to a major historical discovery, and she had fallen in love.

That was the profound change. It had happened overnight, literally. And she knew that it would affect every day of her future. Omar Dukhan was in her heart and in her blood.

And her feelings for him now were just the beginning.

The waiter offered to carry the tray of coffee for her, but Beth declined. She'd just started back to the room when she heard Mauve's scream. The sound held such outrage and horror that Beth shoved the tray of coffee onto a table in the lobby and sprinted up the stairs to Mauve's room.

Out of the corner of her eye she saw John Gilmore come out of the restaurant and Omar come from the front lobby of the hotel. They were both hot on her heels.

"Beth," Omar called, "wait."

But she didn't. Her friend was in trouble. She cleared the stairs and ran down the hall to Mauve's open door. She heard her friend muttering dire curses, and the sound galvanized her to run faster.

"Mauve!" She dashed into the room and halted. Mauve stood beside the computer imager, her hands clenched into fists and her body shaking.

"What in the world?" Beth asked.

"It's destroyed!" Mauve cried. "Someone came into my room while I was having breakfast and destroyed the computer! I'll call the management." She moved toward the phone.

"No!" Beth's answer came instinctively. "Let's be sure someone broke in before we attract any outside attention."

John and Omar halted at the doorway. Beth waved them back as she stepped up beside Mauve. The image on the computer screen wavered erratically, accompanied by a thin, screeching sound.

"How bad is it?" she asked Mauve. Beth knew the principles behind the machine, but she had no idea how to work it.

"It's a total loss," Mauve said, unclenching her fists.

"This wasn't an accident. I tested the computer thoroughly for bugs before we came. Someone did this on purpose." She gripped Beth's shoulders. "Someone is trying to sabotage our excursion!"

Beth knew what Mauve said was probably true. But it could have been equipment failure. "Who?" she asked. "Who would do such a thing?"

John stepped into the room. "Why don't you ask Omar?" he said, pointing at the desert guide, who remained in the doorway. "Ask him," he repeated.

"What are you saying?" Beth demanded.

"I'm saying your *guide* may be more than he appears. I saw him this morning. I thought he was coming from your balcony, Beth. Perhaps it was Mauve's room he'd been visiting. Maybe he was after more than a roll in the hay."

Beth was too slow to stop Omar. His fist crashed into John's face, sending the scientist flailing to the floor.

"Say what you want to me, but don't ever think you can talk to Beth like that." Omar stood over him, fists clenched.

"Stop it!" Beth grabbed Omar's arm and pulled him out into the hall. "Stop it," she said, her voice rough with emotion.

"I'm sorry." Omar touched her hair, his hand as gentle as his softest touch the night before. "I'm so sorry, Beth," he whispered.

"It's okay." She looked in the room and saw that John was getting to his feet. "What was he talking about?"

Omar didn't hesitate. "I climbed onto the balcony

of your room this morning because I thought I heard you cry out. But you weren't in your room, so I jumped back down to the garden. John was lurking in the shadows. I knew then he'd draw the worst conclusion. I was right.''

"You didn't do anything to the computer, did you?'' Beth knew her voice was almost desperate with hope.

Omar brushed her forehead with a kiss. ''I have been in front of the hotel for the past half hour, talking with Abel, the man who is providing the camels for your journey. If you'd like, you can ask him.''

Beth felt as if oxygen had finally gotten into her lungs after minutes of depravation. She could breathe again. She could allow herself to feel again. Her hand touched Omar's arm, slowly moving down it. ''I don't know what's going on, Omar, but I have to figure it out. My backer has been very generous, but that computer was expensive. I'm not certain I can replace it and continue the trip.'' She was unloading her worries on Omar, a man who was in no way responsible to help with them. But just the telling felt good. She didn't dare discuss such things with the rest of the crew. Doubt was an emotion never allowed in a leader. Omar understood this.

"I know your heart is set on finding the City of Con, but without the underwater images, what can you do?'' He didn't wait for her to answer. ''There are other sites, Beth. Other discoveries to pursue.''

Beth heard a strange growling sound and looked past Omar to the door of her own room. Familiar stood in front of the door, tail twitching and a throbbing growl coming from deep in his chest.

"What's wrong with him?" Beth asked.

"Cats are often difficult," Omar said.

"I don't know…" Beth started toward the cat, but Familiar darted away from her.

"Leave him alone," Omar said. "He's fine."

Beth sighed. The cat was acting strangely, but right now he was the least of her worries. She touched Omar's cheek. "I'll meet you for lunch. I think it would be better now if you left me alone with Mauve and John. Once I know how bad the damage is, I'll be able to talk with you about our plans."

"I'll see you at noon." Omar lifted her hand and pressed a kiss into her palm before he left, robes swirling around his long legs.

METHINKS I'VE MADE a horrible miscalculation. Desert Hawk may be too noble a name for the man in the robes. Maybe Oilcan Harry or the Riddler would be more appropriate. I fear I may have helped the villain wriggle his way into Miss Explorer's heart. And all along I thought I was just a kitty in the service of Cupid.

Omar has lied to Beth. He's misled her in a way that she will never forgive him if she discovers it. Why would he do such a foolish thing?

No more time for cogitation. It's time for action.

OMAR HURRIED through the crowded streets. It would have been easier to hail a cab, especially in the heat. But he needed action. He needed movement. He needed exertion to help assuage the guilt eating away at him.

There was no justification for what he'd done. Perhaps he might have been able, one day, to make Beth understand that he had to protect his heritage. He had to honor a sacred vow. But by seducing her, he had crossed a line. His desire for her, his growing feelings for her, had been the very thing that destroyed any future they might have had.

He clenched his teeth. No, that was wrong. There hadn't been a chance for a future. They were two people at odds. The thing that had brought Beth into his life was the thing that had come between them.

He was cursed by the gods. His brother had escaped the curse, but he had taken it up, knowingly. And he had knowingly hurt Beth.

As he neared the edge of the city, the crowded streets gave way to narrower dirt roads with more camels and livestock than cars. He took several turns until he came to a low stone building that seemed to be made out of the very rocks of the earth.

From within the building came a low, throaty whinny.

"Kaf." Omar spoke the word as if it would give him absolution.

He entered the dark building and moved unerringly toward a half door that opened into a large stall. Walking through the stall, he went to a second door, which led to a paddock.

"Kaf," he called to the black stallion.

The horse arched his neck, shook his mane and reared, pawing the air. With a wild cry he came down on all four legs again and ran directly at Omar, head shaking wildly and mane flying.

Instead of stepping aside, Omar stood his ground. Only a foot in front of him the horse stopped. With a low whinny, the stallion used his nose to gently push against Omar's chest.

"So you've missed me," Omar said, rubbing the stallion's forehead. "I've missed you, too. How about a ride?"

He didn't bother with a halter. He simply walked out of the stall into the main aisle of the barn. The stallion followed and stood while he was brushed and saddled.

Omar led the horse into the street and swung up into the saddle. Using the lightest of touches, he turned the horse away from the city and nudged him into a gallop. Within ten minutes the city was left behind, and Omar and the stallion were running free across the sands of the desert.

With the wind blowing in his face and the desert around him, Omar found a few shreds of peace. But even as he tried to outrun Alexandria and Beth, he knew that he would have to return. There was no escaping the future he'd chosen for himself.

HOLDING AN ICE PACK to his face, John sat on the edge of Mauve's bed as the two women began to work on the computer.

"That man is trying to ruin you," he said.

Beth didn't respond. She helped unscrew the cover to the delicate interior of the computer.

"I saw him, Beth. He was on the balcony."

Beth walked to the balcony door and tried to open it. "It's locked, John. How would he have gotten in?" She returned to the computer.

"You'd better check into his background. He may be hired help for a rival group."

The computer cover slipped in Beth's trembling hands, and she caught it just before it struck the floor.

"John, shut up or go to your room," Mauve said, casting a worried glance at Beth. "I'm sure Beth will look into this. Now zip it or leave. We're trying to work here."

"I guess it's too late to call the police. We should have checked for some fingerprints or something."

"We should call the authorities, anyway," Mauve said. "This is an expensive piece of equipment. If it was tampered with, the insurance won't pay unless we go through the police."

Beth was reluctant to draw the Egyptian law enforcement into her business. She'd worked hard to keep her expedition as low profile as possible. Calling the police would be tantamount to taking out an ad in the newspaper. Reports would be filed, reporters would read the reports, stories would be written and read, and then questions would be asked. Lots of questions. Some of them would be directed at the financing of her trip. This was exactly the scenario she wanted to avoid. Nazar Bettina would not like it. Beth didn't like it. John had hit on the fact that a rival or competitor might be responsible for the vandalism. That was entirely possible.

The world of archaeological finds and discoveries, while viewed as scientific and dry by some, was as cutthroat as any Wall Street capitalist group. The stakes were high, the potential for fame tremendous. While most people in the field were highly ethical professionals, there were always renegades and people willing to do anything to win.

"Beth, should I call the authorities?" Mauve asked. She put down the tool she was using to work on the computer.

"Let me think about it."

"Think about it?" John asked, excited enough to jump to his feet. "What's to think about? Afraid your desert lover will be incriminated?"

Beth's fuse was slow and long-burning, but it finally reached the explosive point. "Another word, John, and you're off the team. I mean it. Your animosity toward Omar is so huge that you can't see the rest of the picture. A police report will draw media attention to us. Do we really want that? Is the insurance money worth the risk of having our story spread across the newspaper and on television? You're worried about rival scientists—well, if we manage to get on TV, you can bet there will be at least three expeditions forming by tomorrow. And without that video from the temple, we're not even one step ahead of anyone else."

John sat back down. "I see your point."

"My relationship with Omar is none of your business. But rest assured that I won't jeopardize this discovery for any reason. Or any man."

Beth felt a dull headache crawl from the back of her head toward the front. She normally didn't suffer from headaches, but her emotions were in turmoil and her stress level was almost beyond endurance.

"John, why don't you check with the crew on the boat? Maybe we can reschedule for tomorrow and get back down there," Beth said wearily.

"I'll do that."

He left the room and Beth sank onto the bed. Mauve sat beside her and put an arm around her shoulders. "Don't let John's accusations ruin this for you. Omar hasn't given you any reason to doubt him, has he?" Mauve asked.

"I'm not sure I doubt him. It's just that…I guess I doubt myself. I let him close to me, Mauve. Too close. Now I'm scared."

"Pretty normal reaction, if you ask me." Mauve rubbed her back lightly. "Now prepare yourself for some good news."

Beth looked at her with a question in her eyes. "Good news? Hurry up, I could stand some about now."

"I got most of the images transferred to disk." Mauve bit her lip and raised her eyebrows. "Even better. I got them printed out! The images are spectacular. I've already started deciphering some of them, and they are directions to the City of Con. I'm positive."

"Mauve!" Beth stood up. "Really? How did you do it?"

"I started on it last night, and I got so excited I just kept working. I also thought that if we could transfer the underwater video to digital disc, it would be so much easier to work with in the desert. We could use one of the laptops, instead of the big monster." She patted the computer that had been destroyed.

"Why didn't you tell me sooner?"

"I don't trust John," Mauve said simply. "I don't like him and I don't trust him. He's always accusing someone else of something. That just naturally makes me suspicious that he's the one who's up to something. I think we should keep the existence of the video disk between us for now.''

Beth laughed. ''Now that's female logic if I've ever heard it.''

''Go ahead, scoff. But when I'm proved right, I'm going to say, 'I told you so,' so many times that you're going to think my needle is stuck.''

''I hope you're wrong about him.''

''I'm not. John's up to something. If you have to watch someone, focus on John. As for Omar, he's a keeper. I'd give anything for a man to look at me the way he looks at you.''

''I think I'd be better off if I forgot about men and focused on my work,'' Beth said, meaning it.

''Better off?'' Mauve paused thoughtfully. ''Probably. But happier? I don't think so. I know you're scared, Beth. It's scary to care about someone. But think about what it would be like to have someone in your life who cared about you.''

''Let's get to work,'' Beth said, anxious to change the subject.

''Okay. You're the boss.'' Mauve reached into the drawer of her bedside table and pulled out a sheaf of pages. ''Not exactly the safest place for storage, but if someone wrecked the machine, at least he didn't think to look for hard copy.''

As she took the pictures, Beth felt her excitement build. The first image was a voluptuous female body with a long, thin neck and the head of a regal feline. The catwoman seemed to stare directly at Beth, as if challenging her to unravel her secrets.

"Con," Beth said.

"I don't think there's any doubt that we were in her city temple. I've looked at some of these symbols. They're complex for the period of time they were created, and as John pointed out, it would have been simpler to use the alphabet. Unless, of course, Con was deliberately making this as hard as possible."

"She was a powerful woman, and, as such, was despised. More than one attempt was made on her life. In fact, there were attempts to wipe out her entire tribe. Some said that all the followers of Con had made a pact with the dark side to attain the powers of prophecy."

"Amazing, isn't it? Had Con been a male, I doubt she would have been so persecuted."

"I believe you're right. But had Con been a male, neither of us would be that interested in finding her secrets."

Mauve chuckled. "Good point, Beth."

"Let's see what we can figure out." She began to lay out the pictures in order, checking to make sure each one was numbered on the back. It was going to be a long day with a lot of tedious work. In many instances she and Mauve would be only guessing what the symbols meant. Though some common symbols had been assigned meaning over the ages, no one could be absolutely certain.

"Here we go," Mauve said, pointing to the second symbol, a clutch of wheat held in the claw of some big bird. "Wheat could mean wealth, plenty, harvest, a specific location where wheat was grown..." She sighed. "I need that coffee now."

"That's why I'm paying you the big bucks. Quit complaining and let's make a list of every possible meaning. I'll run downstairs and get the coffee—lucky they have those thermos carafes. When I get back, we'll start checking to see if any symbols are repeated."

Beth was downstairs and back with the coffee in less than a minute. While Beth put cream and sugar in a cup, Mauve arranged the photos on the floor, checking each one to make sure it was numbered in the correct order.

Heads bent together as they knelt on the floor, the two women worked. Neither noticed the black cat that had jumped in the balcony window and sat, perched on the sill, watching first them and then the garden outside.

Chapter Eight

Omar gave Kaf a good rubdown and then hailed a taxi back to town. The ride had done him a world of good. Looking out over the vast stretches of desert, he'd reconnected with his home, with the isolation and joy of his people and the land they had traveled for generations.

He'd done a bad thing, but a necessary thing, when he'd destroyed the computer. He'd done what honor demanded.

Sleeping with Beth was another matter. He could not let that happen again.

He went back to the hotel and slipped into the lobby. Several of the scientists were at the bar, drinking, their worried expressions telling him that the expedition was in serious trouble. Out of the corner of his eye, he saw John approaching. He could stay and have a confrontation, or he could walk away. He wasn't a man who walked away.

"Beth's checking out your background, Dukhan. You'd better be clean or there's going to be a world of grief coming down on your head." John's jaw was swollen.

"My past is impeccable," Omar said. "My credentials as a guide are the best in the business. If Ms. Bradshaw isn't satisfied, she can hire another guide.''

''And she will. Don't worry about that.'' John strode away, leaving Omar standing in the lobby while some of the other scientists stared at him. He was drawing far too much attention to himself.

''Where is Ms. Bradshaw?'' he asked Ray. He saw the man's gaze dart from one to another of the scientists before he answered.

''Upstairs. She and Mauve are trying to fix the computer. She doesn't want to be disturbed.''

''Has she rescheduled the boat?''

''Yes. We're leaving tomorrow at eight.'' Ray sipped his beer. ''Are you going with us again? I'm not so sure that's a good idea. John's taken a real dislike to you.''

''If Ms. Bradshaw wishes, I will be there,'' Omar said. He'd wondered if Beth had the funds to go through the underwater leg of the journey again. Obviously she did. So, the destruction of the computer hadn't stopped her quest, it had merely delayed it. His heart sank. He'd hoped he wouldn't have to take any more measures to halt Beth. Now he knew that he would.

BETH STACKED the photos and gave them to Mauve. ''Did anyone ever tell you that you do good work?'' she said with a big grin.

''Other scientists are clamoring for my help, singing my praises, but I remain loyal to you,'' Mauve said. She wiped the back of her hand across her forehead. ''Loyal, and suffering from a pounding headache. My brain hasn't worked so hard in a long, long time.''

"I know what you mean." Beth, too, felt a vague headache, but nothing overly troubling. "Maybe it's the stress."

"Maybe. More likely it's the three pots of coffee I drank. I know, I know, I shouldn't be such a caffeine fiend." Mauve waved a hand in the air to halt Beth's words. "I think I should lie down for a little while before dinner."

Beth looked closely at her friend. Mauve's normally pale complexion was blanched. The light sprinkling of freckles across her nose, normally barely visible, stood out against the whiteness of her skin. Beth put her hand on Mauve's forehead and then withdrew it quickly. "You're burning up. You have a fever." Concern shot through her.

"I'm just tired," Mauve insisted. "A few hours' sleep and I'll be fine."

"I'm going to call a doctor." Beth went to the phone and rang the desk. In a moment she'd made arrangements for an English-speaking doctor to visit Mauve in the hotel.

"Imagine, a doctor who makes house calls. Maybe we should take him back to the States with us." Mauve stretched out on the bed. "I'm just a little sleepy." Almost before she finished speaking, she was asleep.

Beth's heart was hammering. Something was very wrong with Mauve. Before the team had left the States, everyone had had vaccinations against several different viruses and diseases, but no one's immune system had defenses against every bacteria that might be encountered. It was a danger all travelers faced.

Beth sat by the bed, her friend's hand in hers. When

she heard the tap on the door, she jumped to her feet. The doctor had made excellent time. She stacked the photos in a dresser drawer, swung the door open and halted. Omar stood before her, his white robes a contrast to his tanned face. His dark eyes searched hers, and worry creased his forehead.

"What's wrong?" he asked.

"Mauve is very ill. She had a headache and now she's…asleep." Beth's voice broke.

Omar hurried to the bed and touched Mauve's forehead. "She's burning up."

"I know. A doctor is on the way."

"What did she eat?" Omar asked. He went to the room-service tray that was still on the small table.

"We had some chicken for lunch." Omar was scaring her.

"You both ate it?"

"Yes." She touched his arm. "What's going on?"

"Anything else?"

Beth shook her head. "Wait. Mauve drank several pots of coffee."

Omar lifted the used coffee cup. He looked at the unused cup and at Beth. "You didn't drink any?"

She shook her head. "I get the shakes if I drink too much. I had some in the morning but none this afternoon."

Omar picked up Mauve's half-filled coffee cup and uttered a sound of disgust. "Your friend has been poisoned," Omar said, his lips thinning.

"Poisoned? How can you know for certain?"

"I don't know for certain. But I know the symptoms. Headache, high fever, then sleep, which can soon turn into a coma. Look at this cup.'' He held it out to her. ''Around the edge, see the way it shines?''

''What is it? Will she die?'' Beth asked in a whisper.

Omar met her eyes and didn't answer. Beth's heart blossomed with fear. It seemed impossible that vibrant, healthy Mauve could die.

Omar took her hand, forcing her to pay attention to him. ''When the doctor comes, tell him to treat her for castor poisoning. He may have to hunt to find a pharmacy that has the ingredients he needs. Try my friend, Majaro, at this pharmacy.'' He hurriedly wrote an address on a slip of paper for Beth. ''You must act quickly.''

''Thank you, Omar.'' Beth took the paper just as another knock came at the door. She rushed to open it. A very thin man with round, rimless glasses stood holding a black bag.

''I'm Dr. Rashad.''

''Come in.'' Beth waved him toward the bed and her friend. She heard the door close and looked up to realize Omar was gone. Hovering behind the doctor, she watched as he made a quick, initial examination of Mauve.

''This is very serious,'' he said. ''We need to move her to the hospital for lab work.''

''I think she's been poisoned with a part of the castor plant,'' Beth said.

The doctor's eyes opened wider and he turned to examine Mauve more closely. ''It could be,'' he said. ''Yes. I've heard of this, but I've never seen a case of it. If this is true, time is of the essence. We must get the antidote immediately. If we are too late, she will slip away from us.''

Beth reached into her pocket and pulled out the address Omar had given her. "This pharmacy has the things necessary to make the antidote."

Again the doctor's eyes widened. "You seem very familiar with our city," he said quietly.

"My guide told me this. He also recognized the poison."

"He's a very educated man," the doctor said slowly. "Very educated and very astute. Who is this guide?"

"His name is Omar. Omar Dukhan."

The doctor immediately bent to his bag, snapped it shut and stood. "I will treat her for the castor poison, but we must also get her to the hospital for tests. I can't afford to trust the diagnosis of a desert guide. If it isn't poisoning, then it is some other thing, something that may be the first of an epidemic."

"What can I do to help?" Beth asked. "Mauve is my friend and my co-worker. I want her to have whatever she needs."

"Yes, I'm sure you do." The doctor finally looked at her, his gaze speculative. "Money is a wonderful thing, isn't it? It can buy medicine and treatment, while others have no hope of it." He walked to the door. "I will send an ambulance. Your friend will be taken to Alexandria Medical Center. By the time she arrives I will have the antidote."

His gaze swept over Beth in a way that made it clear he didn't approve of her. Then he was gone.

Beth stood for a moment in the center of the room, wondering just what had transpired.

OMAR STRODE out of the hotel and into the street. He wasn't certain where he was going, but he had to get away from Beth and the very ill Mauve. If help wasn't sought immediately, he knew that Mauve would die.

Someone had poisoned coffee that was meant for both Beth and Mauve. Perhaps solely for Beth, and Mauve was just collateral damage. The poison could mean only one thing. Someone else had found out about Beth's expedition, and that someone meant to stop it. Who? That was the question Omar knew he had to answer, and fast. Close on the heels of that question was another—why? Other than the small tribe of descendants of Con who viewed the city as a sacred place, who would want to stop the discovery? Ancient sites brought many dollars into the Egyptian economy. After the initial exploration and removal of treasures and wealth, the tourist dollars would continue into eternity. Omar knew that most of his countrymen would welcome another "find." Who would not? The first answer was a rival team of scientists that wanted the glory of finding the lost City of Con. That idea made him close his eyes. Was he sabotaging Beth only to let someone else beat her to glory? Someone who went right to attempted murder as a method of competition?

He stopped at a corner and looked around, aware that he was in front of his brother's office building. Lights burned brightly on the tenth floor, and he suspected his brother was still hard at work. Harad had traded his desert life for servitude to money. Omar ground his teeth. His brother belonged in the desert, with him. But Harad had made his choice and would not be persuaded. Now all of the responsibility for protecting his people and his past rested on Omar. He had to honor his family's vow to protect Con and her descendants, to make certain that her holy city remained untainted. He had no choice in the matter. Still, he couldn't help wishing that he could walk into the building and take the elevator to his brother's office, where he could sit down and talk with Harad about what was happening. But he couldn't. He and Harad had begun to rebuild the bond that had once been strong and true between them, but that bond was still fragile. Harad had made it clear five years earlier that he wanted nothing to do with the lost city.

Omar was faced with a difficult decision. He could honor his vow to protect his people by stepping aside and letting fate determine what happened to Beth and her crew. Or he could step into the breach and protect the woman he loved.

It wasn't much of a decision. Beth could not be harmed. Neither could the scientists who worked with her. Stopping her from finding Con was one thing. Injuring her or her friends was something else again.

With that decided, Omar looked up at the office building where his brother toiled. A small degree of understanding touched him. Harad had made a choice Omar didn't understand. It was one he would probably never understand. But Omar, too, had just made a choice that went against everything he ever thought he would do. He'd chosen his heart over his people.

He felt tiny pricks along his leg and looked down. There was nothing near him. The prick came again, this time sharper. A split second later the black cat popped his head out from beneath Omar's robes.

"Familiar," he said, surprised. He hadn't seen the cat all day.

"Meow." Familiar slipped from beneath the robe and stood on the street, looking up at Omar. "Meow."

DESTROYING THE COMPUTER was despicable, but Omar was not involved in trying to poison Mauve and Miss Explorer. I know, because he was out at the stables with his horse.

Who did try to poison Beth? I only wish I knew. And I wish I knew how he, she or they slipped past me. I was on the case. I was watching. I just never thought that someone would try poison.

It's clear to me that Beth was the target. Mauve, God love her spunk, is terminally cute, but she isn't the powerhouse of determination that Beth is. No, someone is trying to stop this expedition from going forward, and they know that Beth is the ticket. Without her, the others would pack their things and return home.

Omar Dukhan is an interesting man. Even more interesting is Dukhan Enterprises, the building before which we stand. I wonder if this is a coincidence. A famous lawman once said that there are no coincidences. Or was that a famous philosopher? Who cares—it rings true. Dukhan may be as common in Egypt as the name Smith is in the States, but somehow I don't think so.

I'm going to herd Desert Hawk back to the hotel. He might tear up a few more machines, but he won't let anything happen to Beth. Then I'm going to do what should have been done before these folks ever left the *good ole U.S. of A. I'm going to run a background check on Omar.*

I'm applying just a little claw to Omar's shin. Yes, it does feel good to torment him. I admit it. I take pleasure in making him hop on one leg. He destroyed the computer and he needs to feel discomfort.

Ha! Folks are stopping on the street to watch him dance around. Since I'm hidden beneath his robes, they can't see me. They think Omar is having some kind of fit. Interestingly enough, he isn't trying to kick me. He's trying to get away, but he isn't trying to hurt me. I can't understand what the people are saying—I must have missed the kitty lessons on how to speak Egyptian in five easy classes. But I can tell by their expressions that they are finding the floor show highly entertaining.

I love this country! Cats are gods! I can claw and torment Omar in the middle of the street, and he can only avoid me. What a place! When I finally hang up my kitty investigator's license, I may consider coming here to retire.

Flapping around in his white robes, Omar looks something like a whirlwind of laundry in a cyclone. Now he's getting the idea. He's going back toward the hotel. He's moving along without any prompting. He's only a humanoid, but he did catch on quickly. I think he may be trainable. Maybe.

He's going in through the garden, which shows he's smarter than your average biped. And, yes, he's taking a position in the shadows. I'll give him a little rub on the ankles and then I'm going upstairs. Beth will be back from the hospital soon, and before she arrives, I want to have that background check done.

Thank goodness Eleanor took that computer class and learned how to do these things. I only hope Beth is hooked up to the Internet. Surely she is. Surely.

OMAR TOOK UP a position beneath the balcony of Beth's room. He had a clear view of the garden and also the staircase that gave access to the second floor, where her room was located.

Though he knew Beth was at the hospital with Mauve, he knew she would soon be back. The cat was right—if it was possible the cat was trying to get him to keep an eye on Beth's room. The first attempt on Beth's life had failed. There would be another.

He leaned against the stone wall, grateful for the coolness. His skin was hot from the long ride in the sun, and the building offered solace. He thought of the oasis upon which the City of Con had been built. It was a small one, by some standards, but plenty to sustain the band of nomads who called it home.

To call it a city was inaccurate. The City of Con consisted of a temple surrounded by the dwellings of the followers. All community business had been conducted in the temple. All worship. All ceremony.

One of the clearest pictures of his early childhood was watching his mother on the steps of the temple, ringing the chime that marked the summer solstice. His mother's job had been mostly ritual, but it was a role she took seriously. So seriously, in fact, that Aleta had chosen her duties over her husband.

It was the same choice that had split Harad and himself. He wondered how his mother would feel to see the same blade slice through her family yet again.

But it was because of Aleta that he had chosen the protection of his people. It was in her memory. In her honor.

Beth reminded him a lot of his mother. Not physically, but in her dedication to her beliefs. Her quest for the lost city was more than a ticket to fame. She wanted to say something about the role of women. Even as he thought it, he realized how much his mother would have approved. Aleta was a feminist, and one who often spoke out, even when the cost was high.

He was still thinking when he heard the sound of footsteps outside the garden. Dusk had begun to fall, but visibility was still excellent. He pressed deeper into the shadows and waited.

Ray and two of the other scientists opened the garden door and stepped inside, closing it carefully behind them. He recognized Judy and another one of the men who'd dived with them, Sam. A robed man was with them, a man Omar didn't recognize.

"Are you sure we should be doing this?" Judy asked. "Beth is going to be upset."

"Beth is going to delay us for days if we have to wait for Mauve to recover," Ray said sharply. "What are we supposed to do while we wait?"

"We're going out to dive again," Judy said. She glanced at the robed man, who seemed to look straight through her to Ray.

"So we dive. Then if Beth isn't ready to head out, we go without her. She can catch up. I'm sure that Omar the Magnificent can get her through the desert to us with no trouble."

"You just want to find the city first," Judy accused. "You want the glory."

"So do you," Ray said.

"What about John?" Judy asked.

"He's not going to say anything. He hates Beth and he hates Omar even more. He'll hop on the first camel we offer him, I guarantee it," Ray said.

"Beth could cut off our salaries," Judy said. "She won't sit still for this."

"If we get there first, what choice will she have but to either embrace us as her expedition or admit that we got there before she did?"

Judy shrugged. "You're assuming we'll be able to decipher the directions and find the temple all in one day. We don't even have the optic-computer now. It was destroyed."

"We have underwater cameras. We can do it the hard way," Ray said. He turned away from Judy. "Either you're in or out, I don't care. Just quit whining."

Ray walked right past Omar and into the hotel. Judy and Sam followed. The robed man was last in line, lingering several paces back. When he went by, Omar grabbed his sleeve.

"You're aligning yourself with dogs," he whispered in the man's ear. "They will cheat you and not pay you for your time. I know them. They are cheating a friend now." He spoke rapidly in the tongue of his people.

The Bedouin looked deep into Omar's eyes. "I know you," he said carefully. "You are a man of your word. Thank you, friend," he said. "I will spread the word."

"Good," Omar said, drawing back into the shadows.

Chapter Nine

Beth returned to the hotel, her only thought a hot bath and bed. Mauve was out of danger and on the road to recovery. The antidote that Dr. Rashad had prepared worked like a miracle. The doctor said he would release Mauve from the hospital in the morning if she continued to recuperate so rapidly.

His words of warning, though, were burned into Beth's brain.

"Your friend came very close to dying. This poison was not meant to make her sick. It was meant to kill."

Beth unlocked the door to her room and closed it behind her, locking it.

"Meow." The black cat stood up on the bed, stretched and jumped down, walking over to rub against her shins.

"Familiar," she said. "I'm glad you're here." At first she'd been unsettled by Familiar's ability to slink through the smallest opening in the balcony window. He came and went into all the rooms at will. His presence had become a comfort to her.

She started running a bath and slowly undressed. She needed to talk to the rest of her team, but she didn't have the energy. She wanted to see Omar, but during the long hours at the hospital, a dark fear had taken shape in her mind. Omar had known the poison. He'd known it immediately. How? And why would he have given the name of the antidote if he'd meant to kill her or Mauve? None of it made sense.

As she stepped into the steaming water, she remembered his touch. The tears she'd held back at the hospital began to trace down her cheeks. She sat in the bath and allowed herself a good cry.

The cat strolled into the bathroom and jumped onto the side of the tub. He licked her with his rough tongue until she slowly gained control of her emotions.

When she finally got out, dried and put on her pajamas, she wanted only her bed and a long sleep.

"Meow." Familiar scratched at the door.

"You want to go out?" She opened the door a crack. The cat waited, the tip of his tail twitching.

"Me-ow!" His cry was more demanding.

"What?" She opened the door wider.

He stepped into the hall and snagged the leg of her pajamas with his paw. Beth followed him into the hall, then down to the door of Mauve's room.

"She's not there," she told the cat.

He paid no attention. He batted at the door with his paw, demanding that she open it.

Beth got the key to the room and opened the door, following Familiar as he went inside and hopped up in front of the computer screen attached to the communication computer. The monitor blinked in readiness in the darkened room.

Curious, Beth slipped into the chair and began to

look at the screen. The Web page devoted to Omar Dukhan made for fascinating reading.

He was the son of Suleman and Aleta Dukhan, members of a nomadic tribe who specialized in the breeding and training of Arabian horses.

The bloodlines of the horses stretched back almost to prehistory, and she scanned through the photographs of the various studs and dams, stopping at last on a black stallion that seemed to vibrate with energy and life. Kaf. The horse was thought to be one of the finest stallions in the history of Arabian breeding.

She scrolled through more pictures, finally coming upon a brief background. As she read, her heartbeat skipped. Omar had earned a degree in botany in Paris and graduated at the top of his class. His field of interest had been native plants used for medicine.

Bracing her hands on the desk, Beth closed her eyes and absorbed the information. Omar knew about the castor plant because he'd studied it. She let her mind go no further than that, but continued to read.

He'd worked briefly for a German company with an office in Alexandria and had quit abruptly in 1999, when he'd begun to hire himself out as a desert guide for tourists.

The information on the Web site continued with facts that Beth already knew about her guide. She scanned through them, wondering how she'd missed all the other things. She'd checked Omar out through a reputable agency. She'd made sure his credentials were good. She looked at the Web site and realized that someone had tapped into a way she'd never heard of to search the Internet.

A chill raced up her spine. Who had been at the computer checking on Omar? John Gilmore popped into her head. John had suspected Omar all along. He'd raised question after question about him, and she'd allowed her emotions to rule her thoughts. Now if John knew this information, he would use it as a way to undermine her authority and judgment with the other crew members.

Her weariness was gone, and in its place was panic. She had to see John. She had to find out how he'd gotten into Mauve's room and how much he knew about Omar.

She was about to get up when the black cat jumped into her lap. Familiar deftly tapped on the keyboard and the Web site disappeared, replaced by a site showing a list of Arabian breeding facilities near Alexandria.

"Familiar," Beth said with awe. "*You* found the information about Omar?"

Familiar's golden eyes blinked once.

"You were checking up on him?"

Again the single blink.

"I'm going to call the authorities," Beth said. "Mauve almost died. He's a botanist. He knew all about those plants and what they could do."

Familiar leaped from her lap and went to the telephone, sitting on it. "Me-ow!" he said, adding a hiss as she reached for the phone.

"I don't believe this," Beth said. "You don't think I should call the police?"

The cat blinked once, then began to purr.

"I must say, you have very clear feelings about this. I'm just not sure I should trust them. Feelings are deceptive," she said ruefully. "I trusted Omar, and look where I am. It's possible he also destroyed the computer."

Familiar looked at the computer in question, but he didn't make a sound.

"I can't take my people into the desert with a man who may be trying to poison us," Beth said, feeling a need to defend herself to the cat.

Familiar blinked twice.

She furrowed her brow. "You're saying he didn't poison the coffee?"

"Meow." The soft cry was followed by a single blink.

"I don't know." She shook her head. "I just—"

A soft tap at the door made her stop in midsentence. Familiar darted down by the side of the bed and Beth followed. One way to find out what was going on was to remain in hiding and see who came into the room.

Cradling the cat in her arms, Beth slipped beneath the bed. She could see the edge of the door and watched as it swung open. In her haste she'd forgotten to lock it.

"Beth?" Omar's voice was soft. "Beth, are you in here?"

She hesitated. He sounded worried, but what did that prove?

"Beth?"

Before she could stop the cat, he darted out from under the bed. She saw Omar jump back.

"You again? What now? First you claw me in the middle of the street, and now you want me to come into this room? What are you up to?"

Beth realized that Omar was talking to the cat as she did—as if he believed that Familiar actually knew what they were saying. For some reason, it made her feel better. Omar came from a culture that revered cats, yet he had taken the respect for the feline to a new level. And so had she.

"Me-ow!" She heard Familiar pounce on the bed with a cry of victory, and she knew that if she didn't show herself, the cat would soon lead Omar to her and she would suffer the indignity of having him find her on her belly beneath the bed.

Slowly she crawled out and got to her feet. Omar was watching with some amusement and a lot of relief. "Looking for something?" he asked.

"You know I'm not. I was hiding. I didn't know who was coming into the room."

All traces of amusement fled. "I'm glad to see you're taking some precautions. How's Mauve?" He crossed to Beth and took her hands. "I've been worried."

"Mauve is going to be fine, but she almost died." Beth gazed deeply into his black eyes. The moonlight came in from the window, and she realized she was talking to a man who could be every woman's fantasy. His lean jaw was gilded by the silvery light, emphasizing the clean lines of his brow and nose. The hint of a beard showed through his skin, adding just a shadow of mystery.

"What was wrong with her?"

"You tell me," Beth said, unable to hide the accusation in her voice.

"Was it the castor?"

"The tests aren't conclusive yet. But Dr. Rashad believes that's what it was. She responded to the antidote."

"Thank goodness," Omar said, tightening his grip on her hands. "How are you, Beth?" He reached out and touched her forehead lightly.

Beth shivered at his touch, suddenly aware that she was standing in very lightweight pajamas. She could feel the effect of his touch on her body and knew that if he looked closely, he could see it. She withdrew her hands and turned away from him.

"What's wrong?"

"You didn't mention that you were a trained botanist," she said, turning back so that she could see his face.

"So?"

"So how many other people would know about a castor plant?"

She saw the effect of her words. They were like a slap. His expressive eyes suddenly turned to stone. "Are you accusing me of poisoning Mauve?"

"I'm saying you haven't told me the truth. How would *you* read it?"

"What would it matter to you that I'm trained in botany?" he asked. "How would that affect my ability as a guide?"

"It wouldn't. But it would give you a leg up in the poisonous-plant department."

"If I had meant to poison Mauve, why would I have given you the antidote?" he asked.

"Sounds reasonable, until I consider that the poison

may have been meant for me. When I didn't drink the coffee, maybe you decided to save Mauve.''

Omar was silent. ''I see.'' He took a step back from her. ''I think you should find someone else to guide you into the desert. Before you do, though, I urge you to use caution. Some members of your party are already planning their own expedition. Ray hired a guide. They're planning on leaving day after tomorrow whether you're ready to go or not.''

Beth sank onto the bed. ''Ray? Who else?''

''Judy and Sam were with him.''

''And John?''

''To my surprise he didn't seem to be a part of this.'' Omar took another two steps back, reaching for the door. ''My advice to you is to stay alert. We have an old saying here. The translation is something like, 'Keep your friends close and your enemies closer.' ''

''We have the same saying,'' Beth said, tired and deflated. ''It's one I've always hated.''

''You have enemies here. Go home, Beth. You'll be safe there.''

Before she could say anything, Omar was gone, the door closing softly behind him.

OMAR LEFT THE HOTEL, aware that John Gilmore was standing at the desk watching him. He heard Beth on the stairs coming after him, and he heard her call his name. He didn't stop. He kept going.

Beth had been right on target to suspect him of perfidy, so why had it been like a knife to the heart? He'd destroyed her computer, which was an act of disloyalty. Was poisoning her friend such a big leap for her to make?

His thoughts tormented him as he walked several blocks in an effort to collect himself. There was only one person he could talk to about the choice that faced him. Harad had already given up the role that now held Omar prisoner. They had faced different choices, but there were many similarities. Omar stopped at a corner bookstore and called his brother's office. In only a few moments Harad agreed to meet him at a small café. Just like in the days of their youth, Harad had asked no questions. He had simply agreed to meet.

Omar walked briskly in the direction of the café. Up ahead, a robed figure flitted into a dark alleyway. Omar noticed, but didn't think anything of it until he passed the alley. Without warning, the man ran toward Omar, a cry of battle on his lips.

Omar saw the knife flash in the moonlight and dodged just in time. He glanced around, aware that the street was empty except for himself and his attacker.

"Who are you?" he demanded of the man in his native tongue.

The man didn't answer. He feigned left, then dove straight at Omar with the knife slashing in an upper cut that, had it connected, would have gutted Omar on the spot.

Omar brought the heel of his hand down on the man's knife hand as he deftly sidestepped him. The knife flew from the attacker's hand, and in a moment Omar had it. He felt its weight and the intricate scroll-work on the handle. Then he gripped it point up in the way of a man who intends to do as much damage as possible.

The stranger crouched, ready to attack. He slowly began to circle Omar. Just as Omar thought he would rush him again, the attacker turned and ran into the alleyway. His footsteps echoed as he ran down it, and when he reached the far end, he half leaped, half climbed a fence and disappeared. Omar opened his palm and looked at the weapon. It was finely crafted and clearly the tool of a professional. It must have cost a great deal of money.

As for the attacker, Omar guessed that he was a man hired to do a job. Among Omar's people, there was a certain honor to a fight. A man was challenged and a time was set. Ambushing an enemy was a dishonorable act. Whoever the man had been, Omar knew that he bore no personal grudge. He had simply been hired to do a job.

Omar went back out to the street and looked around for a taxi. He was surprised when a Mercedes sedan pulled over to the curb and the passenger window rolled down.

Cautiously Omar walked to the car and leaned down. His brother's profile was clear in the moonlight.

"Need a lift?" Harad asked.

"Yes." Omar settled into the passenger seat of the car. The window rolled up automatically and the door locked. Omar held out the knife. "A man just attacked me. He left this behind."

Harad took the knife gingerly. As a young boy, he'd been highly trained in the use of a knife. Now Omar saw that he touched it as if it was something he'd never seen and didn't like. His brother had left the desert far behind him.

"Why are these people trying to hurt you?" Harad asked.

"I don't know for certain," Omar said, "but I suspect it has to do with the expedition I'm guiding."

"The quest for the lost City of Con?" Harad handed the knife back.

"Yes."

"A quest that will end in failure."

"Yes." Omar lowered the knife to his lap. "Now I have a question for you. Did you find out who was backing Beth? If I can cut off her funds, I can stop her without damage to her reputation."

"I have many sources. None of them can provide the name of the backer. Whoever he is, he's very clever and he's gone to great lengths to protect his identity. The question I can't help but ask is why."

"You find it suspicious that this man would not reveal himself?"

"Suspicious is too strong a word," Harad explained quickly. "I'm only saying that he is very resourceful. But I did hear that you'd made enemies. Men who wanted you out of the way but chose not to confront you themselves."

"Who?" Omar asked.

"The scrollwork on the knife will tell you. You have a rival, Omar. Someone willing to hire an assassin to get you out of the way. Use caution, my brother." Harad put the car in gear and pulled into the street. In a moment they were parked in front of the small café

Omar had suggested. Instead of getting out of the car, he looked at his brother.

"Can we save our talk for another day?" Omar asked.

Harad smiled. "You want to talk to me about a choice. The woman or the desert people." He put a hand on Omar's wrist. "I can listen, but I have no answers for you." He touched Omar's chest. "The answer is there. Only you can know it. But I am available to help you in any way. You have only to ask."

Omar knew Harad spoke the truth. No one could counsel him on this decision.

"Where shall I take you?" Harad asked, pulling back into the traffic.

"To the hotel."

"To the woman?"

Omar hesitated. "Yes," he finally said.

"What is she to you?" Harad asked as he drove, his eyes focused on the empty road.

"That remains to be seen," Omar said.

"Only to a blind man," Harad answered. "Just remember, my brother, a man in conflict with himself has already lost the battle."

"Your words are wise," Omar conceded.

"I lost my mother to her ideals," Harad said. "I don't want to lose my brother."

WITH FAMILIAR CURLED at her side, Beth waited out the remainder of the night. She called the hospital twice to check on Mauve. Each report reassured her that her friend was on the mend. But nothing could reassure her that her heart would ever repair itself.

Omar had not denied her veiled charge. He had not denied anything. He had simply offered her a few worn adages and disappeared. Good riddance! If only she could believe that. And he had warned her about a mutiny among her own crew. What was she going to do?

Nazar Bettina had funded her expedition because she had assured him that she could provide top-notch professionals who would take care of their responsibility. Now it was abundantly clear to her that each and every one of the scientists on the trip had his or her own agenda. She had suspected this of John Gilmore. She had been aware of Ray and Judy's doubts about her theory regarding Con. Still, she had not expected betrayal.

The morning sun found her wide-awake, her fingers stroking Familiar's silky hide. She arose and dressed. To keep the crew from finding out about the disk Mauve had made, she hadn't canceled the boat she'd chartered to return to the underwater city.

All her crew anticipated a return to the underwater search. She went over her budget carefully and thought over her options. She could send Ray, Judy and Sam out on the water with John, although she hated to leave John if he was unaware of their betrayal. While they were gone, she could begin the overland leg of the journey herself.

She had the pictures Mauve had provided. She had a better chance of reading them accurately than any of the other scientists. Even if they found the temple again, the odds that they could figure out where she'd gone were slim. Of course, she was going to have to do without the expertise that John and Ray and Judy brought to the exploration. But she'd worked sites almost on her own before. She could do it again. It was far better than working with a traitor.

And she would find another guide. At the thought of Omar, tears stung her eyes. Angry with herself for such weakness, she fought them. She might never understand his motives, and she had to convince herself that she didn't care. Mauve had almost died. She couldn't chance another near fatality.

She rose from the bed and went down to the desk. In a few moments she had the telephone number of a reputable agent. After ten minutes of conversation, she'd made an appointment to meet with another desert guide for early the next morning.

She put in a call to the number Nazar Bettina had left with her. She had only bad news to relate, but she felt duty-bound to keep him abreast of all developments. The phone rang repeatedly, but there was no answer.

She hung up and placed a call to Amelia in New York. Much of her eager enthusiasm for this adventure was gone, but she still had to let her "sister" know where she was. And she wanted the comfort of Amelia's voice, her wisdom. To Beth's bitter disappointment, the answering machine picked up again. Amelia's silky voice promised to return her call as soon as possible.

"I'm in Egypt, Amelia," Beth said, forcing her voice to be vibrant and full of energy. "I'm on the adventure of a lifetime. You wouldn't believe it, but I'm searching for the lost City of Con. Remember, I told you about the goddess. I'm in Alexandria right now, but I'm headed out to the desert in a day or so. Things are really hectic. I'll try to call back and let you know what's going on. I love you. Bye.''

With that accomplished, she went to Mauve's room and gathered the printout of the hieroglyphics and the disk. She couldn't risk leaving them around. She found the soft leather pouch that Amelia had given her for a Christmas present and packed the material inside it.

Now. She was ready to go downstairs. If the members of her crew wanted to play games, she'd be glad to oblige.

Chapter Ten

Beth was seated in the lobby when Ray, Judy and Sam came down carrying their diving gear.

"How's Mauve?" Judy asked.

"Do you really care?" Beth answered. She saw the look of guilt the three exchanged.

"Of course—" Judy began.

Beth cut her off. "The dive has been canceled." She spoke in an arctic tone that silenced the protest Judy started to make.

John Gilmore had joined them, his own gear stacked by the door. "What do you mean you've canceled the dive? We can't go forward without the directions, and since someone destroyed the optic computer—" he gave Ray a hard look, as if it had suddenly occurred to him that Ray was capable of such an act "—we don't have anything to work with. We have to go back down there."

Beth kept her voice calm, though she was furious. "In case you haven't heard, John, some of our co-workers have hired their own guide. They were going to let me pay for the boat and the dive, then steal the information they gathered and head off into the desert on their own, while I stayed here to make sure Mauve was not going to die.''

John didn't say anything, but the expression on his face indicated that he, too, had been kept in the dark about this underhanded plan. It did her good to realize she'd driven a wedge between John and the others. But that didn't counteract the sense of betrayal she felt that the team she'd handpicked had been on the verge of leaving her behind with a sick friend.

She looked at Ray and Judy. ''If you want the information beneath the sea, put together your own expedition and backing. And get your own equipment. That belongs to me.'' She motioned to the porters she'd already paid. The men stepped forward and began gathering the expensive cameras and equipment, moving them to the hotel's security room.

''Beth, we felt we had to move fast,'' Ray began.

''So fast you couldn't even fill me in, Ray? I don't think so. I don't think you had any intention of telling me about this, except maybe by telegram when you'd found the city and designated yourself as the great archaeologist. In fact, I know that to be true.''

''How can you be so sure?'' Ray challenged.

''Your guide is fluent in English. You should keep your plans to yourself next time you try to double-cross your employer.'' She was getting angrier by the second, and she wondered how much longer she could control her temper.

''We would have cut you in on the deal once you caught up with us,'' Ray said. ''Did he tell you that?''

''Not in those exact words. I believe it was something to the effect that I wouldn't have a choice. I could participate in the find or admit that my own team had beaten me.'' She saw that her words hit home. Omar had overheard the entire conversation and given it to her in true detail.

What did surprise her was the look of disgust on John Gilmore's face. It was almost as if he disapproved of Ray's tactics. Beth felt, though, that given the chance, John would behave in exactly the same way. The recognition of the find was too great. The temptation for those who sought glory and fame was irresistible. They would step on any and everyone who got in the way.

In that second she understood Omar's concern for the secret treasures of his land. She saw the truth behind his worry. No matter how good her intentions were, once she made the site of the lost city public, there would be others stampeding over Egypt wanting glory and fame no matter the cost to the local people.

She'd worked with Ray and Judy for the past five years. At the excavation site in New Mexico where they'd unearthed traces of a little-known Indian tribe, she'd shared the limelight of discovery with both of them. Not once, as head of that team, had she taken all the glory and cut the others out.

Her repayment was their betrayal. Along with Sam, whom they'd recommended to her, they hadn't even hesitated. As soon as they saw an opportunity, they'd tried to dump her and move forward on their own. They would have stolen her expedition—the journey she'd dreamed about and worked for more than four years to put together. Adding to her fury was the recollection of how Ray and John had scoffed at her idea of a lost village ruled by a woman with the powers of a goddess.

"I hope you guys have fun finding a ride back to the States," Beth said as she pulled all of the return airline tickets from her bag. "It seems I'm holding all the return tickets, and they've all been paid for by Bradshaw Enterprises. Oh, seems I have all the passports, too. I'm sure you can get another, but it will take some time and effort."

Judy blanched. "Hey, you can't leave us here without passports. We won't be able to get home."

"Oh, yes, I most certainly can," Beth said. It would give her pleasure to leave the three scientists stranded. They could get new identification, but it would be a major inconvenience. It would also open the door to a lot of questions. Somewhere along the line, someone would ask why she'd left them stranded in Alexandria—why they'd been fired.

She enjoyed the scene in her mind before she reined in her imagination. "I can inconvenience you any damn way I please. And I may take your passports and throw them in the sea. I haven't decided. Right now, I'm on the way to the hospital to check on Mauve. Remember her? She's your co-worker who almost died." She didn't bother to hide her sarcasm and was rewarded to see all of them lower their gazes. At least they had the decency to be ashamed of themselves.

"What are you going to do?" Ray asked.

"I don't know." She had to think it through. In just a few short hours she'd lost her guide and half her research team. Could she possibly continue with half a crew?

"I assume you can't go anywhere until you get those hieroglyphics out of that underwater temple," Ray said.

"I wouldn't assume anything," Beth retorted. "You know what they say about assuming. You've already proved you're unethical, Ray. Don't prove that you're an ass."

She'd had enough. She walked past them and out to the street, where she hailed a cab. Around her, Alexandria was awaking, and it was a city of intense energy. She could smell the spices from the market that was a block away. Cinnamon, curry and others she couldn't readily identify. It was a heady mixture, and it instantly brought to mind the dark-eyed Bedouin. At the thought of Omar she felt first hot, then cold. He'd taken her to a restaurant where the spices were so well used by the chef that she could only sigh in pleasure.

And then he'd taken her to bed.

The memory made her flush as the cab careered through the streets. It had been the most intense sexual experience of her life. Just the memory of the way his hands had moved from her waist down her hips, the way his eyes had held hers when he touched her, brought a rush of desire for him.

Omar.

And now he was gone.

She felt the emptiness in her heart and quickly hardened her emotions. She knew what loss felt like. Knew intimately. And she also knew that it was something that weakened and crippled those who succumbed to it.

There was no place in her life for weakness. All

around her were sharks and barracudas. Co-workers who would eat her flesh if she showed a sign of weakness. No, she would not think about Omar.

At the hospital she was relieved to find Mauve already dressed and waiting.

"I'm starving," Mauve said. "Can you believe it? I'm almost killed by poison and all I can think about is eating something else."

Beth hugged her friend. "I think that's a wonderful sign. How about a traditional Alexandria breakfast?" She wanted to talk to Mauve about what had happened with the crew, but she wanted to be sure she was strong enough to take it.

"What is a traditional breakfast here?" Mauve asked a little skeptically.

"Who knows? Let's find out," Beth answered as she escorted her friend out of the hospital and into the waiting cab. "We'll find something to eat just as soon as I mail a package to my sister." She pulled a tiny padded envelope from her purse. "I'm sending Amelia a disk and a copy of the prints of the hieroglyphics. It's just a bit of insurance. I told Amelia about the lost city and the sabotage. If anything happens to me, Mauve, go to Amelia Corbet. She'll be able to help."

"Good," Mauve said. "Someone besides us needs a copy of that information. Just be careful. I don't know who to trust anymore." She leaned back against the seat as the cab sped away.

"Amelia is totally trustworthy. Better than that, she's a powerhouse. If anything happens to me, you call her." Beth patted Mauve's arm. "Things are going to be fine. We'll find the lost City of Con."

Beth reached across the seat and pointed at a delivery service. She told the driver to take her there and wait. As she got out, she looked at the small package. It was everything she'd told Mauve—and more. In the return address, she'd used not her own name, but Merlin. It was part of a childhood secret code she and Amelia had used to communicate. Beth no longer knew whom to trust in Alexandria. She needed her sister. And as soon as Amelia saw that one word, she'd be on her way.

Beth filled out the forms, paid the fee and returned to the cab, feeling as if a weight had been lifted from her shoulders.

AH, MY LITTLE Miss Explorer has a spine. She took it up with those creeps she hired and made them eat their grits. Now they're all wandering around the hotel trying to figure out how to get home. I guess they didn't think Beth would do to them what they tried to do to her—abandonment. Well, I think it's good enough for them. Maybe they'll think twice before they try a stunt like that again.

I must say, I thought Omar would have hung around, though. He's gone, I suppose. I guess a guilty conscience got the better of him. Destroying the computer was wrong, but he evened the score by telling her what Ray was up to. Now he can disappear back into the desert with a new group of tourists or whatever it is he does.

I just didn't think he would. I saw the way he looks at Beth. He's in love with her, even if he is too thick-headed to know it. What gives with humanoids? They

*write and read and go to great pains to prove they're
learned and smart. And yet they are so disconnected
from what they feel. It's almost as if they've been
trained not to acknowledge their feelings, so they just
deny they feel anything. They gird their loins with pride
and stoicism and keep putting one foot ahead of the
other. What a waste. It would serve them far better if
they sat down somewhere quiet, like on a pillow in the
sun, and tried to figure out what was actually happening in their heads and hearts.*

*Like Omar storming off last night. Nothing but con-
flicting emotions. He was ashamed of himself for trash-
ing the computer. So when Beth, reasonably enough, I
might add, pointed out his botany training and
Mauve's poisoning, his pride was wounded. Had he not
already done something unethical, he might have been
able to talk with Beth about her allegation. But no,
pride and guilt are a lethal cocktail to rational conversation. He just got up on his high horse and rode
off into the sunset. Now all I can do is wait and see.*

*I've been playing the role of tourist a bit. I love this
city. There's something happening on every street. I've
been watching the exquisite kitties. It's fascinating to
see them saunter around while humans accommodate
them. For example, a cat starts into the street, and
voilà, the cars slow and stop. And when a cat passes
on to the next life, the humanoid caretaker shaves his
or her eyebrows off. Cool!*

*The result is that these cats have an arrogance that
I greatly admire. I wish I had a video camera so I could
bring some footage home. Clotilde would love it. She's*

always harping on the fact that she's a superior puss, as of course she is.

I'd better quit lounging around here and check out a few leads. I'm a working kitty, not one of these Egyptian feline gods. Then again, none of these cats has his own PI license. It would be terrific to be worshiped, but I guess I'm just an American kitty at heart.

Omar left mad, but something tells me he'll be back. Beth needs him here. I have a bad feeling that the dirty tricks have only just begun.

I'll scout the perimeter and hope that Desert Hawk is somewhere, keeping an eye on things.

OMAR RUBBED a hand over his face, aware that he desperately needed a shave. He'd been awake all night, watching Beth's room. His anger had sent him into the street, where he'd nearly been killed. Concern for Beth had sent him straight back to the hotel. He gave a rueful grin as he realized he'd bounced back and forth from the hotel like a puppy chasing a bone. And Beth Bradshaw was the one tossing the bone.

He'd chosen the garden as his lookout point, reasoning that if anyone tried anything, they wouldn't go down the hallway but would attempt to slip in through the balcony door, as he had done.

As pink light filtered over the city, turning the walls of the hotel from shadow to a luminous white, he slipped the knife he'd taken from his attacker out of his belt and examined it closely. Harad had touched the knife with true aversion. His brother had left behind his desert training on the quick and lethal use of such weapons. But was it an aversion to knives in general

or this knife in particular that had made Harad so uncomfortable?

Omar felt the balance of the weapon in his hand,
touched the blade that was honed so sharply it would
slide through muscle and bone with little pressure. The
jewels on the handle made it particularly valuable. This
was the elegant weapon of a professional assassin, a
man who killed for large sums—or simply because he
enjoyed the act. The question Omar had to determine
was why *he'd* been targeted. Was it something relating
only to him, or did it have to do with his association
with Beth?

His gut told him that the latter was more likely.
Someone had already made a serious attempt on Beth's
life.

He'd gone over and over the poisoning in his mind
and ruled out Beth's employees. Unless they'd brought
the poison with them, he didn't believe they'd have the
resources to buy it in Alexandria. There was plenty of
poison to be had here, but the sellers were leery of
foreigners, especially Americans. He'd made a few
phone calls, though, and maybe one of his sources
would turn up the buyer.

Activity at the front of the hotel caught his eye, and
he shifted position so he could watch Beth hail a cab.
She was going to the hospital. Soon she and Mauve
would return to the hotel. Then he would learn what
their plans were. It still stung him that Beth suspected
him of trying to kill her.

Killing her was the last thing on his mind. Stopping
her was another matter.

He went into the dining room and ordered coffee,

his gaze following the other scientists as they huddled at a corner table. He could tell by their expressions and the arguments that erupted among them that Beth had lowered the boom on their plans. He couldn't suppress a grin at the thought.

He felt a hand on his shoulder and, though startled, didn't flinch. Slowly he turned to look at John Gilmore.

"Did Beth tell you what happened?" the man asked.

"Yes." Omar saw no need to tell John the exact exchange of information.

"She's canceled the dive."

"Oh." He kept his voice noncommittal.

"If she's planning on heading into the desert without some directions, she's insane. People have been hunting for that city for centuries, and they've never even gotten close."

"That's a good point." Omar studied the scientist. His gray eyes were flecked with worry. Or was it desperation?

"Why do I always feel like you know more than you're telling me?" John asked.

Omar shrugged one shoulder. "I can't answer that."

"Why did you take this job?" John pressed. "You're not a desert guide."

Omar smiled. "You've caught me out, John. My name is Bond, James Bond." To his surprise the scientist smiled back.

"Okay, so I'm a little paranoid and a big worrier." He took a seat at the table. "Beth is too trusting. She hired those guys over in the corner even though I warned her not to. Ray is insane with jealousy when it comes to her work. Judy will side with anything in pants, and Sam is just a follower.''

"And what are you?'' Omar asked.

"I argue with Beth and I challenge her authority, but we've worked well together over the past years."

Omar watched the shift of John's eyes and wondered if that was true. "What can I do for you, Mr. Gilmore?''

"Convince Beth to leave those traitors behind. She gave them an earful this morning, but I know her. By the time she gets back, she'll have forgiven them and she'll let them continue on with us. It'll be tough, but we can make it without them."

"Are you sure Ms. Bradshaw will continue? She lost the hieroglyphics that will direct her to the city. She's canceled the return trip to the underwater temple. Perhaps she intends to pack it in and return home."

"Ha! You haven't been around Beth for long. She'll die crawling through the sand before she admits defeat. It's odd. Beth has always viewed herself as someone lacking in courage and strength. She doesn't even have a clue how tough she is. But she's nails, Omar. Nails."

"Your assessment is accurate," Omar said, wondering if John's concern for Beth was sincere, or if he had another agenda.

"Will you talk to her?" John asked.

It was the opening Omar wanted. Standing in the darkness, he'd realized that though he was no longer Beth's official guide, he couldn't allow her to brave the elements of the desert without him. Even without the lurking presence of someone trying to harm her, the desert was a vast and dangerous place.

"Why do you think Beth will listen to anything I have to say?" Omar asked, playing for time.

"She'll listen to you. Trust me on this one."

"I will speak with her, though I'm not certain my words will have any effect."

John stood up. "If she's determined to go forward, convince her to leave the traitors behind."

Omar gave one nod. "I will tell her of the dangers of traveling through the desert with those who can't be trusted."

"I knew I could count on you," John said, stepping away. He glanced at the table of scientists, who were all watching him and Omar.

"John, one question," Omar said softly.

"Yes?"

"These traitors. Are they so desperate for personal glory that they would kill?"

John's eyes hardened. "Kill? What are you talking about?"

"The poison that Mauve ingested was meant for Beth."

John started to speak, then didn't. He looked over at the table in the corner. "Do you have proof one of the others meant to kill Beth?"

"I'm asking you what you think."

"Greed and jealousy are always part of an expedition, but murder is something else, Omar. It just doesn't seem possible..." He took a breath. "All the more reason to leave them behind."

"I'll speak with Beth." Omar handed John a plain business card with his name printed on it and an address. "Tell her to meet me at this place at ten o'clock. Tell her to wear riding clothes. There's something she should see that might change her mind."

Chapter Eleven

Beth got out of the cab at the sand-colored, stucco building. The sun was hot, but as soon as she stepped into the shade, she felt the temperature drop at least ten degrees. In a land of no trees, shade was a valued commodity.

The business card she held gave no indication of what the building might house. Her first inclination had been not to come, but John said Omar had asked her to meet him. While her brain had urged her to ignore the meeting, her heart had finally won out. Holding a small leather pouch, she stood in the shade of the building in jeans and boots, wondering where to go next. Afraid to leave the prints of the hieroglyphics at the hotel, she had them in a leather valise in her hand.

The sound of a soft whinny drew her deeper into the shadows. She stepped past the doorway and found herself in a cool interior where several horses looked at her curiously.

Her gaze drifted down the row of stalls, stopping at a magnificent black horse who tossed his mane and snorted at her, as if daring her to come closer.

"Kaf," she whispered, recognizing the horse from

the photograph she'd seen on the Web site. The picture hadn't done him justice. He was so nearly perfect that she thought for a moment she was dreaming him.

Step by slow step, she walked toward him. Dancing and shaking his head, he challenged her again. She stopped to stroke the nose of a beautiful bay horse that nudged her gently, demanding her attention.

"Hey, sweetie," she said, rubbing the horse's forehead.

There was a loud sound of a hoof against wood, and she saw that Kaf was pawing at his stall door, demanding attention for himself.

She walked down and put her hand out for the stallion to sniff. He was an arrogant animal, proud and vain. He nuzzled her hand, then snorted, flinging his head up and down as his thick forelock tumbled over his eyes. He looked as if human hands had never touched him. Or as if he had been taught to accept human dominance, but on the inside remained wild.

Then Kaf nuzzled her chest, almost knocking her leather case from her hands. Surprised, Beth stepped back.

"Don't let him fool you—he's gentle as a kitten."

Omar's voice was soft and only a few feet behind her. Beth turned around slowly, unable to stop the painful leap of her heart into her throat. He was unbearably handsome, and the heat in his eyes seemed to sear her. Involuntarily her hand reached out to touch him. Just in time, she forced it down to her side.

"John said you wanted to talk to me."

Omar lifted an eyebrow. "Then he delivered the

wrong message. I told him I wanted to show you something."

Beth glanced back at the horse. "He's truly incredible."

"Kaf is incredible, but that isn't what I want you to see," Omar said with some humor.

"I have work to do, Omar." She shifted the pouch to her other hand nervously.

"This relates to your work."

Her interest was tweaked, but before she could ask another question, Omar went to the stall of the bay horse and led the mare out.

"Do you ride?" he asked.

"I took lessons with Amelia. She was always the better rider. She had nerve and I didn't."

"You only need trust to ride Leah. She'll take care of you." He handed her the halter. "Among my people, our horses are the most effective of watchdogs. Horses have keen eyesight and smell, and the Arabian is the most intelligent of all breeds. If a stranger comes, the horses tethered outside our tents alert us."

"And what dangers lurk out in the desert?" Beth asked. Omar's conversation was never pointless.

"Many." He patted Leah's withers. "The brushes and saddles are up there." He pointed to the end of the barn.

Before Beth could decline, he slipped a halter on Kaf and led him out of his stall and toward the grooming area.

To her surprise, Beth found herself following Omar and Kaf. She'd had no intention of riding. None. And then she realized that she was lying to herself. John had told her to wear riding clothes. She'd worn exactly that. She'd come chasing after Omar, hoping to spend some time with him. The horses were simply an added bonus.

Her old riding lessons served her well as she groomed the mare and put a lightweight saddle on her back. It was neither English nor Western, but a cross between the two. She finished tacking up only moments after Omar, and he looked at her with surprise.

Holding Kaf's reins, he crossed to Leah's side and checked the girth to make sure it was tight enough. "Perfect," he said. "Shall I help you mount?"

The thought of his hands on her waist was enough to call up other images, and Beth felt her cheeks heat. Since the night they'd spent making love, Omar had not mentioned the intense passion they had aroused in each other. What had been an incredible experience to her had obviously meant nothing to him. A night that had changed her life wasn't even worthy of his comment.

"I can manage," she said stiffly. She busied herself with tying the pouch tightly to some leather thongs on the back of the saddle.

Omar looked at her for a long moment, then swung up onto the stallion. He nudged Kaf forward, out into the hot sun, without turning around to see if she followed.

Beth mounted, glad to find the mare as steady as Omar had promised. She found the saddle extremely comfortable, and put on her sunglasses.

Omar didn't bother with conversation. He kicked Kaf into a ground-eating trot and headed away from

Alexandria. Beth rode a few paces behind, giving her body time to adjust to the rhythm of the horse. It didn't take long. Within five minutes she was posting easily and was almost at Kaf's tail.

"Where are we going?" she asked.

Omar slowed until she drew up beside him. Kaf arched his neck and preened for the mare.

"To a special place. I think you'll like it."

"Tell me, Omar, is this part of the guide package?" She couldn't constrain the bitterness in her voice.

He turned in the saddle to study her. "No, Beth, this is just for you. A special gift."

"And why would you want to give me a special gift?"

"I'm wondering that myself," he answered, not bothering to hide his annoyance. "Perhaps you'll learn something that will be of value to you."

"Why do you care?" she continued. She was a fool, an idiot, and she was laying out her heart for him to stomp on.

"I've asked myself that question," he said softly, reining Kaf to a slow walk. Leah fell into pace beside him. The stallion swung his head over and nipped the mare's neck. Squealing, Leah struck out at him with her front leg. By simply touching the stallion's shoulder, Omar corrected Kaf's behavior.

"He's flirting with her, and she's playing hard to get," Omar explained. "They can play their games in the paddock, but not while they're being ridden."

They rode in silence, and Beth became absorbed in the landscape that spread before her. The paved road had given way to dirt, and in the distance she could see that either the sand had swept over it, or the road simply ended.

When they reached this spot, they stopped, and for the first time Beth realized how vast the desert was and how easy it would be to get lost. The view was the same in every direction. There seemed to be no landmarks, no way of charting a course except by the sun and stars. She was struck with a true appreciation for the Egyptians' scientific study of astronomy.

"With the exception of some military vehicles, from this point, travelers must go by horse or camel," Omar said. He nudged Kaf into the sand. "Arabian horses have wide, well-shaped hooves. They've evolved physically to meet the demands of their environment." He readjusted the loop of his reins. "So have the people of the desert. We've changed to adapt to the great demands of the place we love."

Beth listened intently. Omar had something to tell her, but he wasn't going to come right out and say it. It was up to her to decode his words.

"I can see how someone would love this place," she said, acknowledging the sweeping hills of sand that seemed to roll in the distance like gentle waves. She'd imagined Egypt, but she'd never come close to grasping the power of the land.

"My family has lived in the desert for many, many generations. My forebears worshiped the ancient gods and bred horses. I tried another life, but I came back to this. There was really no other choice. My people needed me." He patted Kaf's neck. "We have been struggling for the last three generations. Kaf, though, is going to change that for us. He is not only a magnificent horse, but he can produce equally magnificent sons and daughters. He is the heart of our new breeding program, one that will attract interest from around the globe. In order to do that, I've had to learn to live both in the desert and in the city. I've had to learn to wear suits and to walk among the men of business. I've had to learn the high cost of deceit and betrayal.''

Beth felt her pulse speed up. ''I know that price, too.''

Omar turned to her, his gaze holding hers for so long that Beth felt the heat rise in her body. She didn't want to feel desire for him. She despised herself for such weakness.

''I didn't poison your friend,'' Omar said at last. ''You have my word on that.''

They stared into each other's eyes for a long, silent moment. Heart pounding, at last Beth nodded slightly. ''I believe you.'' And she did. Foolish or not, she believed him.

Breaking his riveting gaze, she looked at the sweeping dunes. Then she looked back at Omar and knew that in this moment she was truly seeing the man he was. She'd never seen him so at home. He was where he belonged, and she suddenly realized that she had never felt that way. She'd lived in many places, but she'd never belonged anywhere. She was always a transient, moving from one site—one dig—to the next.

''I envy you,'' she said softly. She swept a hand in front of her. ''This is truly your home. You know where you belong.''

''There is a price to be paid for every decision. To know my place has cost me greatly.''

"What do you mean?" Beth sensed that this was what Omar had brought her into the desert to tell her. This was the crux of the matter, if only she could figure it out.

"If you don't belong anywhere, then you don't have any place to defend."

The words were spoken with such sadness that Beth put her hand on his leg. She'd touched him in comfort and was unprepared for the sexual charge that tingled up her arm and into her body. She pulled her hand away, but not before she saw the same charge in Omar's eyes.

He swallowed, his gaze moving from her lips to her breasts and finally away. "Give Leah her head," Omar said, leaning forward in the saddle. "She'll stay with Kaf."

Omar squeezed his legs around the stallion, and Kaf burst forward. Leah was right at his hip.

Beth felt a jolt of apprehension that was almost instantly replaced by sheer joy. The two horses galloped through the sand, stretching out and running. There were no barriers, no roads or cars or worries. There was only the sun and the sand and the powerful surge of the animal beneath her, and as Beth gave herself to the primitive sense of freedom, she laughed out loud.

Smiling with pleasure, Omar cast a look at her. "You ride well," he called back to her, notching Kaf's speed up a little.

Beth didn't bother to answer. She'd never been a bold rider, but her trust in the mare was absolute. She felt no need to try to control the horse. She simply wanted the sensation of flying across the sand. Leaning down into Leah's neck, she let the mane whip against her face.

Twenty minutes later, when the horses slowed of their own volition, Beth wiped away the tears the hot wind had whipped up in her eyes.

Omar turned to her. "Riding in the desert is like no other experience."

"I've never felt so free," Beth said. "Thank you, Omar. It was a special gift."

He reached over and brushed a strand of hair from her cheek. "That wasn't the gift. There's something I want to show you." He pointed due south, and Beth could see what looked like some sort of bluff.

"What is it?"

"An old tomb."

"Whose tomb?" She was surprised.

"The person it was created for was never a ruler. And it was never used as a tomb. In fact, it's of little archaeological significance, but the story there is one I thought you might want to hear."

Once again, Omar was talking in code. He was going to give the clues and allow Beth to unravel the real meaning. She clucked to Leah and followed Omar across the sand at a trot, her gaze on the bluff, which wavered in the distance like a mirage. By her guess, the tomb was still several miles away.

Distance was impossible to gauge. The sand dipped and rolled around them, and Beth's estimate of the distance was left far behind as the horses continued to trot while the tomb shimmered in the distance like a mirage.

Although they kept a steady pace, the horses were tireless, their sweat drying in the hot breeze.

Beth thought her eyes were deceiving her when she saw what looked like greenery. "An oasis?" she asked.

"Yes, very small. Because it's so close to Alexandria, it isn't of importance to travelers and isn't often used, except by my people."

"You know every inch of this land, don't you," Beth said.

"It is my home."

"It's different in America."

"If you had ever found your home there, you would know it inch by inch." Omar pointed to a speck on the horizon that seemed to be moving toward them.

"What is it?" Beth asked. The heat seemed to shimmer in waves that distorted her vision, but it appeared to be a man on horseback headed her way.

"It is Yemal. He's one of my best riders."

"You can't possibly identify the rider from this distance." Omar was impressive, but he didn't have X-ray vision.

He laughed at her. "Of course not. But I know that Yemal is riding the outskirts of the oasis today. Therefore it stands to reason that unless he is sick, that is him."

Beth gave him a wry smile. "Logic."

"A trait I've heard is sorely lacking in women."

Beth was surprised at Omar's wit. She could tell by the lift of one dark eyebrow that he was deliberately trying to get a rise out of her.

"That sounds like the statement of a man who hasn't had a lot of exposure to women," she countered, pleased to see the corners of his mouth lift in an appreciative smile.

"Perhaps you speak the truth," he said.

His tone was suddenly so serious that Beth wasn't certain where he'd take the conversation.

"I've always believed that fate would guide me to the one woman who should share my life. I suppose I haven't *practiced* for that meeting as some men do. I trusted that when I met her, the art of loving would be natural." He stared directly into her eyes. "As it was with us."

Beth felt as if lightning had struck her. She stared into Omar's eyes and saw a flash of desire. Before she could respond, he squeezed Kaf's sides, and the stallion leaped forward. Beth held her ground as she watched the desert guide and the incredible horse fly across the sand toward the distant rider.

Leah danced in anticipation of another run, but Beth held her at a walk. She needed a moment to think. Had she heard Omar correctly? Was he saying that he felt she was the woman fate had in store for him?

The possibilities whirled in her mind at dizzying speed. With Omar Dukhan, she was out of her league. She'd dated and had crushes on men, but she'd never felt the tidal wave of emotion and passion that Omar generated in her. Up until this moment, she'd believed the emotions were all one-sided. But he'd just said that he felt as if destiny had brought her into his life.

What did that mean?

Beth couldn't fathom it. Omar had directly confronted the issue of the poison, and he'd sworn he wasn't responsible. She believed him. But was it because she wanted to trust him? Because she was already in love with him?

Beth saw clearly the potential for disaster. If she let her heart rule her intellect, she might endanger not only herself, but all the people who still trusted her with their safety and their lives, and Nazar Bettina's money.

OMAR LET KAF open up as they raced across the sand toward the rider, who was also galloping hard. It was indeed Yemal. Omar recognized the youth by the way he sat in the saddle.

Though he tried to focus on the approaching rider, his mind was back with Beth. He clenched his jaw at the memory of his words. They'd slipped out of his mouth, and now he was left with the consequences.

He'd never intended to tell Beth what he felt for her. Just the opposite. His intention had been to convince her that she should rehire him as her guide and then to keep a safe distance from her. Yet his feelings could not be contained.

Watching her ride, he'd taken pleasure in the joy in her eyes as she galloped beside him across the sands. She'd seen the haunting beauty of the land. She'd responded to it, and to the freedom of the ride. Those were things a person could not fake.

And Beth was not the kind of woman to fake or pretend on any level. She was decent and honest and…perfect. He had not lied to her about his inexperience with women. Though his brother had made a career out of dating beautiful women, he had not. Harad enjoyed the game of dating. Even as a young man he'd flirted and enjoyed the challenge of the dance between the sexes.

Omar, though, had not enjoyed the game. In his own quiet way he'd looked for the woman who would complete his world. In his heart he had known that one day he would find her. And now he had. It was a bitter trick of fate that she was set on a course that would destroy his people.

Worse than that, it was cruel irony that he had found the one woman he could love completely, and to save his people he would have to betray her.

He cursed his weakness in speaking his heart to her as he let Kaf thunder across the dunes. He saw it for what it was—an act of cruelty that would only intensify his betrayal.

By the time he was in hailing distance of Yemal, he was thoroughly disgusted with himself. It was only the frown of concern on the young man's face that made him put aside his own self-recriminations.

"What's wrong?" Omar asked the breathless rider before their horses had even slowed.

"Someone attacked the oasis this morning." Yemal spoke in short bursts as he tried to catch his breath. "Thank goodness you've come back."

"How bad?" Omar asked, his gaze searching the young man for injury and then gliding past him to the dim outline of desert tents in the distance.

"Several of the men are hurt."

"Shot?" A tide of anger and worry crested in Omar's chest.

"No, beaten. It was thieves. They came in military vehicles early this morning. We heard them of course.

They drove to the camp and got out. The pretended to be looking for horses to buy. Then without warning they started beating us. They took twelve mares.''

"Horse thieves?" Omar was incredulous. "Horse thieves in military vehicles?"

Yemal nodded, his brow furrowed as he glanced from Omar to the stallion. "They took the mares, but they came for Kaf. They knew all about him."

Chapter Twelve

By the time she'd covered half the distance to the men, Beth could clearly see that something was wrong. Omar waited for her as Kaf danced beneath him. The young rider turned and headed back to what looked like a tent settlement. A thrill of excitement went through her. She'd read a great deal about the nomadic tribes who lived in the desert, and now she was about to see one firsthand.

The expression on Omar's face stopped her, though, as soon as she got close enough to see it.

"My people have been attacked. Some of our horses have been stolen." His gaze swept past her, searching the distance. "They have a head start, but we will find them." He motioned for her to follow him as they rode at a brisk pace toward the settlement.

As they drew closer to the oasis, Beth took in the beauty of the green trees against the azure sky and the rolling sand. No camera could do justice to the sight.

The tents of the tribe were red-and-white striped, a colorful display beneath a stand of palms. Scattered among the tents were beautiful horses. They stood untethered, completely content with their close link to the humans who cared for them. Farther from the tents, a herd of camels were kneeling in the sand.

"Yemal said they stole a dozen of our best mares," Omar said as they stopped at the edge of the settlement. "I was bringing Kaf out here to breed the mares who were in season. Our plan was to sell the foals next year. They would have brought enough money to buy food and supplies for my people for a year."

Beth watched in awe as women and children began to come forward to greet Omar. Their love and affection for him was clear in their actions and their faces. The men waited at a distance, but it was easy to see that they greatly respected Omar.

"What are you—some kind of chieftain?" she asked in a joking voice.

Omar's smile was tight. "Yes, I am their leader, and not a very good one. My people have been robbed and injured, and I wasn't here to protect them."

"You're the leader of these people? What title do you have?"

"In my tribe, the male leader is Connar."

"I've researched the majority of the nomadic tribes, and I've never heard of that," Beth said.

"We are a very small tribe, hardly worth noting in any written studies. We travel with our horses, breeding and trading. We have not been a tribe that anyone would take notice of, but that will change once Kaf gains national prominence as a stallion."

She heard the pride in his voice, and also caution. He was a man who took no chances on the future. "Connar. What does it mean?" she asked.

"The man who carries the bright lamp to show

the…way.'' Omar shook his head. ''I should have been here. I might have prevented this attack. My people, though cautious, are friendly. Yemal said the men came into the village and asked to see the horses. They came as buyers, not thieves. I should have been here.''

''You can't be in two places at once,'' Beth pointed out reasonably. ''You were bringing the stallion.''

He nodded once. ''A very *logical* conclusion.''

A tall, slender woman in her fifties approached. Her gaze swept over Beth, but it was Omar who captured her full attention. Placing her hands on each side of his face, she brought his head down so that she could kiss his cheek.

''Welcome back, Connar,'' she said softly. ''We are in sore need of your guidance.''

''Keya, this is Beth Bradshaw,'' Omar said, stepping away from the woman and giving her a pointed look. He pulled Beth forward. ''She is the head of the expedition I'm guiding to search for the lost city,'' he said.

Beth didn't think it was a good time to mention that Omar was no longer the guide for her trip. In fact, it wasn't a good time to say anything at all. Keya was staring at her as if she were a piece of mouldy cheese.

''Who was injured?'' Omar asked, breaking the tension that had grown between the two women.

Instead of English, Keya answered in a native tongue. Beth could understand only that she was naming names and corresponding injuries.

''Thank you, Keya,'' Omar said, bringing the conversation back to English. ''I'll look at the horses now.'' He took Beth's arm and led her toward a lovely gray mare.

''Who is she?'' Beth asked.

''My cousin. She is my mother's younger sister's firstborn. Were it not for me, she would be leader of my people.''

''Omar, I realize that family runs deep, but isn't this leader thing sort of an honorary title these days?'' Beth's studies of contemporary nomadic tribes had indicated that modern society had had an impact on tribal structures.

''In most tribes, yes. In ours, we retain the old ways. The word of the leader is law. All must obey.''

Beth's eyebrows arched. ''That's a lot of power.''

''And a lot of responsibility,'' he said. ''Now let me see what horses are missing.''

She kept silent as he examined each and every animal that remained in the settlement. When he was done, he turned to her. ''They were very knowledgeable horse thieves. They took the twelve best mares. We have no choice but to get them back.''

''How?'' Beth asked.

''We will find them and then we will take them.''

She couldn't help herself. ''A simple plan, unless they decide they don't want to give them back.'' She was unprepared for the harshness in Omar's face as he turned to answer her.

''They will have no choice,'' he said. ''They will return my horses, or they will die.''

So, MISS EXPLORER has taken off for a desert ride with the desert guide and left me behind in Alexandria. How poetic. I can only trust that Omar will select a nice, gentle equine for Beth to ride. I'm not all that happy about their tête-à-tête in the desert, but it does leave the door open for me to do a little super sleuthing.

Omar Dukhan has a brother who is a big wheel in the push to develop Egypt. When Harad dropped his baby brother off at the hotel, I was able to get the registration number of his car. Even better, I was able to follow him—right to Dukhan Enterprises. Sort of difficult to hide an office building this modern. Harad Dukhan has his finger in a lot of pies, and I'm just wondering if archaeological exploration might not be one of them.

The two brothers are polar opposites. Omar is the man of the sand, and Harad is a walking ad for the Financial Times. I'm thinking sibling rivalry. It wouldn't be the first time that competition between two brothers got way out of hand.

Even so, poisoning an American citizen is a bit extreme.

The only thing for a black cat with dark suspicions to do is check it out. Man, I just love this country. I walk up to the door of Dukhan Enterprises and the doorman opens the door for me. I am a god in this country. My every whim is satisfied by the first human who crosses my path. Oh, my, the doorman is offering me a plate of food! Seafood, too! My favorite!

I'm on a tight schedule, but I'll take a few moments for some sustenance. I always work better when my tummy is full. After all, fish is brain food. Everyone knows that. And I'm going to need all my brain power to find out what Harad Dukhan is up to.

Mm-mmm. This is delicious. Some type of white, flaky fish I don't recognize. Wonderful. And I'm even getting my back scratched while I eat. I hate to eat and run, but I guess I'd better get on the job.

Let's see. Harad Dukhan's office is on the tenth floor. Now I just have to convey to the doorman that I'd like to take a ride on the elevator.

He's pretty smart for a humanoid. He caught on right away. He's moving his hand slowly over the elevator buttons, waiting for me to tell him which floor.

"Me-ow!"

He punched the tenth floor, just as if I'd had him in training for years. Yes, he is highly intelligent for a humanoid. He acts as if he's been punching elevators for a cat all his life.

Ah, here we are. Tenth floor. Am I lucky or what? The door is open and I'm headed into Dukhan Enterprises. Whoa, baby! This is a classy place.

Persian carpets, sculptures, French-provincial furniture that looks authentic. And I recognize those paintings. One is a Monet and the other a Renoir. A little surprising to see European decor and artists, but it shouldn't be. Harad Dukhan has fought as hard to eradicate his culture from his life as Omar has clung to his. Psychologically this is fascinating territory. What could make two children reared in the same family take such different routes? I wish Eleanor was here. She'd be able to figure it out.

Uh-oh, I've been spotted by the secretary, a perfect look-alike for Miss Moneypenny. Hey, she's smiling at me. And she's petting me. Now she's calling out to Omar's brother.

"Harad, you can relax. Tut is home now. He just came in."

"Excellent, Miss Wilson. Give him some cream and tell him that we've been worried about him."

The voice came from another office. That must be Harad's private den. I'll saunter back there as soon as I sample a little of the cream. The fish from the doorman was magnificent, but I am a little dehydrated. The sun, you know. A kitty has to keep up his fluids in this climate. And this is delicious cream. There seems to be a penchant in this country for goat product, but this is heavy cream from a cow. Quite tasty.

Now I'll just— Yikes! Either I'm looking at myself in the mirror or I've got a doppelganger. And he's giving me a very unhappy look. Now I understand why everyone has been so nice to me. It's a case of mistaken identity. This black bad boy must be the roaming Tut. Well, he's proved that you can come home again, and he's caught me sitting in his high chair, eating his porridge and getting ready to sleep in his bed.

I think I'm going to have to do a lot of explaining, and fast.

OMAR STOOD OUTSIDE the tent where he'd made Beth promise she would eat something and rest. He had a feeling she wasn't going to do what he'd told her to do. It was a situation he'd never faced before. In his tribe, everyone did as he said. Even the women.

"Watch her closely," he told Yemal. "She's very smart and she'll try to trick you."

"She won't get out of the settlement," Yemal promised. "But what about you? Where are you going?"

"I want our horses back, and I intend to get them."

"Don't leave me behind," Yemal begged.

"I'm not going after them now," Omar promised him. "Later. Now I want to follow the tracks before they become lost in the sand. I think I know where they'll take me, but I want to be sure before I take a raiding party that far out."

"Promise you won't try to go after them alone," Yemal said.

"You have my word." Omar remembered the scroll-work on the knife that had been used in the attack against him. He couldn't be positive, but he was developing a pretty good idea of who might be behind the attack and the theft of the horses.

Yemal nodded. "The thieves weren't part of the army. They didn't have uniforms and they were dirty."

"Hired thieves," Omar said. "They've been kidnapping tourists and making trouble for the past two years. This time they've made a mistake.

"Keep watch on Beth. She is very important to me."

"She's very beautiful," Yemal said. "The other women are jealous of her. The young ones and the old. The young ones hoped you would select one of them as your wife, while the old ones thought you might take their daughters. Be careful, Connar," Yemal said, smiling. "The women in the tribe are much more dangerous than the horse thieves."

"I think you are wise beyond your years," Omar said, squeezing his shoulder. "Protect Beth. She is my heart."

"Protect yourself," Yemal said. "A woman can inflict more damage than a knife in the gut."

Omar laughed out loud as he walked off into the afternoon heat.

BETH SAT AMONG the soft pillows and beautiful fabrics that had created a luxurious dwelling in the middle of the desert. She'd read all about the tents of the nomads, but she'd never expected to find one so comfortable. The heavy material seemed to block the heat of the sun very effectively.

A horse neighed just outside and Beth realized that Omar had stationed Kaf to watch over her. She was flattered yet still annoyed. Omar was going to do something, and he hadn't shared his plans with her.

Under the guise of protecting her, he'd made her a prisoner. The more she thought about it, the more chafed she felt.

She heard Omar talking with the young man who'd ridden to meet them. Yemal, that was his name. Omar had left him sitting outside the door of her tent. He was the guard for her prison. Well, he wasn't going to be able to keep her confined. Omar had no right to treat her as if she were a child.

Pushing herself up from the pillows, she was about to leave when the tent flap opened to reveal Keya. The tall woman was at the head of a procession of three younger women. They all wore the traditional robes of the desert. Although their heads were covered as protection from the sun, their faces were fully revealed, and Beth could see they were all beauties.

"We thought you might desire a bath," Keya said, indicating the tub and hot water the women had brought.

"That's very thoughtful," Beth said, "but Omar will have to take me back to the hotel soon. If I clean up now, I'll just get dirty again on the ride back to Alexandria."

"You won't be going back to Alexandria today." Keya motioned the young women to fill the tub. "Omar must retrieve the horses. His honor and our future are at stake."

"I have to get back to Alexandria. I have important—" She stopped at the look of amusement in Keya's face. "Where is Omar?"

"He's proposing to go after his horses."

"Does he know who has them?"

"He suspects," Keya said.

Beth refused to let the woman's haughty demeanor intimidate her. "I'm sure Omar will file charges with the authorities once we get to Alexandria. The police will take care of the matter."

"Perhaps that's what Americans do," Keya said with some malice, "but here a man settles his own affairs. He doesn't wait for the police to deal with horse thieves."

Beth started to respond, but thought better of it. Keya seemed to be trying to get a rise out of her, and the worst thing she could do was argue. She was a visitor here. Neither Omar nor the women who were busily preparing her bath would appreciate her comments.

When the bath was ready, the women stepped back, waiting. Beth hesitated. "Thank you."

"Would you like some help?" Keya asked. "It is our custom to make our visitors welcome."

"I think I can manage on my own," Beth said.

"We will wait for your clothes, then. They will be washed and cleaned for the morning."

"But—"

Keya produced a beautiful robe. "You can wear this." She looked at the blue garment and then at Beth. "Blue is Omar's favorite color."

Reluctantly Beth took the robe. "Thank you," she said. "I'll bring my clothes to you." She wasn't about to undress in front of anyone.

Keya smiled. "As you wish." She turned abruptly and left the tent, the other women following her.

Beth stood for a moment, aware that somehow she'd failed a test.

Although she hadn't planned on a bath and didn't want one, the hot water looked tempting. Unaccustomed to riding, her muscles were beginning to complain. The hot water would help her relax and soothe away some of the soreness.

Beth quickly disrobed and slipped into the bath. The water had been scented and softened by oils. She leaned back and sighed. Maybe Keya was trying to be helpful. Maybe the past incidents in Alexandria had made Beth overly suspicious.

She closed her eyes and the interior of the tent disappeared, replaced by a vivid image of Omar racing across the sand on the back of the stallion. She'd memorized every detail—the stuff of fantasies. Omar Dukhan was like someone who had crept out of the pages of *Arabian Nights*.

In this settlement, his word was law. Such power was almost unheard of in the world in which she lived. Leaders came and went at the whim of the electorate.

Here, Omar had been born to his title and his power. And as he had pointed out, his responsibility. So why had he chosen to leave his tribe and guide an expedition into the desert? The horses were his stated means of providing for his people. Why had he become a guide?

The question nagged at her as she rose from the water and began to dry herself. Her skin, softened by the oils, felt refreshed. Outside, the sun was baking the land, but the tent was incredibly cool.

She looked at the plush pillows and thought about a nap. What could it hurt? Omar was busy, and he'd made it clear that his best interests would be served if she remained in the tent and stayed out of the way. A smile touched the corners of her mouth as she thought about what the people of the settlement must think of her. Omar had gone to Alexandria and returned with an American. A female American. The entire tribe was probably buzzing with the gossip.

She slipped into the blue robe and took a deep breath as the material skimmed over her skin. Cotton. Pure, Egyptian cotton. There was no finer fabric in her mind. The bed linens and bolts of material made from the cotton that grew by the banks of the Nile commanded high prices in the United States. Running her hands down the luxurious material, she understood why.

When she turned around, she caught her breath. Keya stood only four feet away.

"I came for your clothes and to give you some wine and cheese," the woman said, holding out a tray. The ruby wine caught the filtered light of the desert and glowed.

"Thank you," Beth said, forcing back the angry words that rose to her lips. She didn't like being startled, and she had the feeling that Keya enjoyed doing that to her.

"My cousins live along the banks of the Nile. They grow the grapes and press them for wine. I hope you approve."

Beth took the tray and set it on a small table beside some pillows. "Where is Omar?"

"He's ridden into the desert. He wants to be certain he knows the direction the thieves took before the wind erases their tracks."

"I see." Beth tried hard to hide her worry. "He went alone?"

Keya nodded. "He's like that." She walked farther into the room and paused, turning slowly. "Since his brother left us, Omar has chosen to spend many hours alone. He has become a solitary man."

"And why did his brother leave?" Beth asked. She found it hard to carry on a normal conversation with Keya. It was as if the woman was taunting her.

"He didn't tell you?" Keya smiled. "Of course, you are his boss, not his woman. I don't suppose he would tell you of his family."

"When will he return?" Beth asked, deliberately changing the subject.

"Whenever he has finished." Keya shrugged. "It could be hours. Or it could be days."

Beth started to protest. She had to get back to Alexandria. She had an expedition to salvage. Mauve was out of the hospital, but she wasn't completely well and she was depending on Beth to return. Beth stopped herself, though, unwilling to give Keya the satisfaction of seeing her frustration.

"Please ask him to come and speak with me when he returns," Beth said.

"Drink the wine. Relax. All will come in good time," Keya said, picking up the goblet and handing it to Beth. "It is the finest wine we have in our settlement. I know Omar would want you to have the very best."

"Thank you," Beth said, taking the wine and sipping. "It's very good."

"Whatever your needs, please let me know." Keya began gathering Beth's clothes. "Omar would be displeased with me if I failed to make you comfortable."

"Everything is fine," Beth said, taking another sip of wine to keep the angry words back in her throat.

"I'll send more wine." Keya slipped out of the tent as silently as she'd come.

Beth drank more of the wine and sat down to cut a wedge of the white cheese. Tasting it, she found it sharp and delicious. Since there was nothing else to do, she ate and drank. It seemed she'd only just finished when a great weariness came over her. She leaned back into the pillows and closed her eyes. She'd rest for just a moment. Five minutes, and then she'd get up.

But her arms and legs grew too heavy to move. By the time she realized she'd been drugged, she was already slipping toward the inviting oblivion of sleep.

Chapter Thirteen

Uh-oh, the jig is up. Harad and his homely secretary are looking at me with deep, dark suspicion. Tut, for his part, has settled on the number-one kitty ploy—he's going to ignore me. I can't say as I blame him. I wouldn't want some look-alike interloper showing up at Eleanor and Peter's pad.

So now it's up to me to make a move. A nice big purr, a little rubbing on the crisp crease of Harad's very expensive trousers. Ah, he's smiling at me. I have won his heart.

To throw them off the track, I'll settle and curl for a kitty nap on his lovely sofa. He's watching me, but making no attempt to stop me. Yes, this is going to work, after all. And he's turning back to the mountain of paper on his desk. It is exactly that mountain I intend to climb. I just have to bide my time.

I actually could stand a nap. Cats, with our incredibly powerful brains, need at least sixteen hours of sleep each day. Eighteen is the perfect amount, but sixteen will do in a pinch. It seems I haven't slept a full night since I got to Egypt. That's the way it is when

I'm working a case. I'll be old before my time. Now that Tut, he's stretched out and already sound asleep.

Harad is getting up from his desk. He's going to confer with his secretary. Now's my chance. I have to be very, very careful. I'll start with the stuff on top of his desk. A casual perusal. I'm not sure what I'm looking for, but I'll know it when I see it. Tut is watching me. He knows that I can decipher the humanoids' language. Will he blow the whistle on me if he figures out I'm looking for something specific? Thank goodness, he's blinking those golden eyes. Sleep is upon him. Another late-night party animal bites the dust. Sweet dreams, handsome prince. By the time you awaken, I'll be outta here.

Let's see, some blueprints for another modern building, some contracts for materials, notes, figures... None of this pertains to anything I'm interested in.

I'll dig a little deeper into the stack. And what's this? A file with Beth Bradshaw's name on it. How interesting. Is Harad looking into Beth on his own? Or for his brother?

The file contains a bio, a list of projects she's worked on, the members of her expedition with a few details about each one. I don't like it that Harad is examining Beth, but there's nothing harmful here.

He's acquired an extensive background on her. He's underlined that she's an orphan and that the Corbet family serves as her kin. That shouldn't trouble me because Beth is so open about her past. But it does. Why would Harad underline that particular tidbit? Something to ponder once I blow this joint.

Here's a bit of history on the legend of Con. Proph-

etess, seer, mystic—none of this is new. There's some handwritten notes on the back. Let me see. Harad really needs some lessons in cursive. Judging by his handwriting, I'd almost guess he was a doctor.

This I can read, though. "She must be stopped." My kitty blood is running cold. Those words are underlined three times. I get the distinct impression that Harad isn't a man who fools around.

I need to get out of here. Beth has gone running off into the desert with Omar, and I'm not certain that's smart. The two desert brothers are up to something. My gut tells me that Beth may be a pawn in a deadly game.

My little kitty whiskers are tingling. Someone is watching me. I'll just stretch and take a look. It's Tut, drat his handsome hide. He's watching me like the Sphinx. And I don't think he's real happy that I'm spying on his human.

I'll just pretend to ignore him and saunter on out of here. I'm going, going—gone! I don't have time to wait for the elevator. If I can get the door to the stairwell open, I'll take the ten flights down.

OMAR SAT ACROSS the low table from Keya. He held his anger in check, but just barely.

"Whatever gave you the idea to drug her?" he asked.

Keya shrugged. "You said you didn't want her making trouble. I thought it was best to make sure she didn't. She isn't harmed, Omar. She's only asleep."

"And she'll awake with a thousand questions. None of them will be good for our people."

Keya suddenly leaned forward. "Our people be damned. None of her questions will be good for *you.* She will think you ordered the sleeping potion in her wine, and you're afraid she won't trust you. You're afraid of the consequences if she thinks that of you."

Omar gritted his teeth. "Why does that offend you so, Keya? Why should it matter to you what my relationship with this woman is?"

"She isn't one of us. She's American. What could she ever really know of our people, our history?" Keya's lips thinned. "Our future. Are you so besotted by her that you'd trade our future for her?"

Omar's hand was startlingly fast. He reached across the small table and grabbed his cousin's wrist. "For the past five years I've led our people wisely. It isn't your place to question my motives."

"She wants to find the lost city. She wants to bring cameras and lights and tours to our sacred temple. How can you even think of letting such a thing happen?"

"You have no way of knowing what I think," Omar pointed out. "You acted without thought, Keya. Don't do it again."

"Or what?" she taunted. "What can you do to me that you haven't already done?"

"What are you talking about?"

She abruptly stood up. "What would you have me do with your little princess once she awakes?"

"Treat her with kindness," Omar said slowly, "if you can find any inside you."

Keya made a sound of disgust. "You should be more concerned with getting our horses back than with a woman."

"Our horses will be returned. Never doubt that." Omar withdrew the knife with the scrollwork and held it out to his cousin. "Do you recognize this?"

Keya didn't take the knife right away. For a long moment she simply looked at it. At last she took it, then got up and moved to the open doorway of the tent where the light was better. She turned it first one way, then another.

"It is from the people of Cemen."

"Yes, I know," Omar said. "Do you think it possible that the horse thieves came from the tribe of Jordel Cemen?"

"Why would Jordel send thieves to beset us?" Keya asked quickly. "He, too, is a nomad. He knows how difficult life is on the desert."

"Yes," Omar said. "Jordel is a nomad, like us. Like us, he has started breeding fine horses. Perhaps he needs some new blood in his line."

"And the knife?" Keya asked. "How did you come by it?"

"I was attacked. Someone tried to kill me in Alexandria. The assassin was carrying this knife."

"Assassin?" Keya slowly sat back down at the table and faced her cousin. "Omar, who would do such a thing?"

"I don't know," Omar said, his gaze holding hers. "I was hoping maybe you could tell me."

"Me?"

"Did you tell Jordel he could have the horses if he got rid of me, Keya? You've always wanted to rule. Were it not for me, you would be the ruler."

"I want to rule," Keya agreed heatedly. "I deserve

to rule. I am female. You are just a man, and yet the blood right was passed to you.''

''That eats at you, doesn't it, Keya,'' Omar said softly.

''Yes!'' She stood up again and began pacing. ''It gnaws at my gut day in and day out. I'm the female. I'm the one who should lead our people. Con's descendants have always been women.''

''Not all of them,'' Omar argued reasonably. ''There was another male ruler of our people. Remember your history.''

''I know my history. I also respect our *traditions*.''

Omar ignored the jab. ''How many dreams have you had lately, Keya?'' He knew her weakness. Keya didn't dream. Not at all. It was something that troubled her greatly. To be a granddaughter of Con and not dream was a curse.

''You have become a cruel man,'' Keya said in a low voice. ''I would never have thought that of you, Omar. Strong, yes. Unbending, perhaps. But never cruel.''

''I am only what I have to be,'' Omar said, wondering how far he would go to carry out the pledge he'd given his mother. Had it been left up to him, he would gladly have stepped aside and let Keya rule. She was strong and brave, and she cared about the village. Yes, stepping aside would have been a blessing for him.

Keya left his tent and Omar wearily lifted the goblet of wine. He sniffed it first before he drank. Keya might slip a sleeping potion into Beth's wine, but she would never dare attempt to drug him.

He savored the taste of the wine. Many of the desert people didn't drink alcohol. His years in Paris, though, had given him an appreciation for the grape. He took another swallow and sighed.

It was almost dusk. Before he could return Beth to Alexandria, he had to get his horses. He'd followed the tracks in the sand until he was fairly certain where they headed. Jordel Cemen was encamped some ten miles away. There Omar was certain he'd find his horses. What he wasn't certain of was Jordel's reasons for taking them.

Reasons, however, didn't really matter at this point. He would weigh motives when he had more time. His first priority was to get the horses back before Jordel uprooted his camp and disappeared into the vast desert. Then he was taking Beth back to Alexandria.

He had a sudden thought. He'd brought her out here to see the tomb. There was a legend involving the ancient site, one that had never been explored. It was risky to show Beth the secret place, but unlike the lost city, this site was not sacred. It had special meaning and contained important secrets, but none that threatened his people the way revelation of the lost city would. He was taking a big risk, hoping Beth might be sufficiently interested in this location and that she'd give up on the lost city.

The chance was slim, but desperate times called for desperate measures.

As the sun began to set, the night grew increasingly and rapidly chill. He decided to check on Beth before he did anything else. It was just an excuse to look at her, and in his heart he knew it.

Beth had become both his greatest pleasure and his most burning pain. His mind told him to behave one way, but his heart—and his body—gave other orders. Just as now. Cool logic told him to stay away from her. His feet seemed to move of their own volition, steadily drawing him to the opening of the tent. Someone had gone in and lit several lamps. Keya, no doubt. She wouldn't hesitate to drug Beth, but she also provided the small luxuries. Beth wouldn't awake in a dark, strange place. At the thought of his cousin, Omar felt the muscles of his back tighten. While he understood her anger and bitterness, he couldn't tolerate her mean actions. Too much was at stake.

All thoughts of the problems of leadership left Omar's mind as soon as he slipped into the tent. Beth was asleep on her side on a pile of pillows. He noted the blue robe she wore. Keya had brought it to her, he knew instantly. His kin was both taunting him and tantalizing him. Keya knew that he would find Beth irresistible in the blue of the robe. It was his favorite color, yet it also heightened Beth's American qualities. She was a foreigner in desert garb, and had he harbored the dream that she might become otherwise, he saw clearly that she would always be different from his people.

She moaned and rolled over, revealing her soft, pliant lips. Omar could almost taste them. Beth was such a contradiction. He'd watched her work with her crew. Though she was never harsh, she was always firm and in charge. She embodied the independence that he so greatly admired in men and women. Yet when she was in his arms, she molded herself to him. In her desire for and need of him, she became the lover every man dreamed of.

Beth moaned again, and Omar, though he'd intended only to look in on her, stepped closer to her bed. Her dark eyelashes fanned out on her cheeks. The soft arch of her eyebrows reminded him of the gently spread wings of a falcon. In the lamplight, her skin took on a peachy glow.

Before he thought, he ran his knuckles lightly across her cheek.

"Omar?" she whispered, reaching up and catching his hand. The smile that touched her features was his undoing. It was pure pleasure. Absolute delight that he had returned to her.

"Beth?" He eased down beside her on the pillow. His heart was pounding. If she went back to sleep, he'd leave. "Beth?" he whispered again, leaning down so that his breath teased her skin.

"Omar, where've you been?" she asked, tugging at his hand. "I was waiting for you and I fell asleep." She blinked her eyes open, but they were still slightly unfocused as she smiled up at him.

"I never knew anyone who could make sleep look like an art," he said, his fingers tracing her hairline and running through the thick mahogany sheaf of her hair.

"We should ride back to Alexandria," she said. "No one knows where I am."

"You're safe," he said, wanting more than anything to make that true.

Beth roused herself, suddenly more awake. She looked around the room, searching for something.

Whatever it was, she found it and settled back against the pillows.

"What time is it?" she asked.

"Night is falling. We can't go back tonight. In the morning we'll rise early and return."

"The tomb? You had something to show me," she reminded him.

"Yes," he said. "Tomorrow. I'll get Yemal to tell you the legend. He's a far better storyteller than I am."

"Another legend?" Beth asked, pushing herself so that she sat up on the pillows. Her brown eyes were focused, and she was slowly becoming more and more aware of her surroundings. Omar could see from her expression that she almost didn't believe she was in a Bedouin tent.

"One you'll enjoy."

"Did you find the horses?" she asked, suddenly remembering the past events.

"Yes. I know where they are."

"When we return to Alexandria, we'll contact the authorities." Beth was watching him closely. He knew someone had told her that calling in the law was not the Bedouin way.

"Everything will be taken care of," he said.

He started to rise, but Beth reached out a hand and touched his knee. "Don't go after the horses. Let the authorities handle it, Omar. I believe you're a man of your word. Tell me that you won't do anything foolish."

The concern implied by her simple words made his heart pound. "It's important that you trust me, Beth. That means trusting my decisions." He knew the words rang with hypocrisy. He could taste the bitterness on his tongue. But in matters of her safety, he wouldn't betray her. He would take care of her, and she had to believe that.

"I do trust you. But I have a question. I've been thinking about Mauve. Who do you think poisoned her?"

"I have someone checking on that," Omar said. "I don't believe Mauve was the intended victim."

Beth nodded. "You think I was. You said that earlier."

Omar hesitated. He didn't want to tell her this, but at least he could be honest in everything but the lost city. "I believe the poisoned coffee was meant for you, but I'm no longer certain for what reason. I have enemies. There are men who wish me harm. Since the theft of the horses, I've been considering what might be going on. Was the attack prompted to stop your expedition, or was it meant to stop your association with me?"

"I'm not sure I understand. I mean, I know what you're saying, but what makes you think this?"

He pulled the knife from his belt of his robe. Holding it out in the palm of his hand, he allowed her to take it.

"This is beautiful, and very old," Beth said, bending to look at the scrollwork. "What a magnificent piece." Excitement tinged her voice. "Where did you get it?"

"An assassin attacked me. He tried to kill me with that knife." He couldn't help a rush of gratification as Beth dropped the knife onto the pillow and grabbed his arm.

"Are you hurt?" she demanded.

"No, I disarmed him and he fled. He has lost much honor by leaving his weapon behind. These are often family heirlooms. Or else they are purchased at great cost. Some of the knives have histories attached to them. They tell the story of a tribe's history. The moments of defense, of revenge, of victory."

"And what story does this knife tell?" Beth's hands remained on his arm. He could feel her fingers gently caressing his muscles.

Omar picked up the knife. "I'm not certain. I believe it belongs to the tribe of a man I once called friend."

"Why would he want to kill you?" Beth asked. She leaned forward, and in doing so brought her soft breasts into contact with his arm. He felt shockwaves all through his body.

"That's the question I must ask him."

Beth tightened her hold on his arm. "When?"

He smiled at her, knowing that yet again he was not going to tell her the truth. "When the right opportunity presents itself."

"And the horses?"

He shrugged. "If he has them, he will take good care of them." He hesitated, knowing that once again he was going to soothe her worries. "I will get them back soon enough."

Relief showed in her eyes. "Then you aren't going out tonight bent on revenge and…" She didn't finish.

"Even if I wanted revenge, I am the leader of my people. I must make the decisions that protect them. Revenge is often a costly passion," Omar said. He didn't add that so was love.

The light of the lamp was reflected in Beth's eyes, and Omar couldn't seem to stop staring into them. And as the lamplight flickered in the depths of her irises, he was startled to see the future.

He saw Beth, dressed in the robes of the desert, walking out of a tent toward a magnificent black colt. The young horse reared and frisked as it ran toward Beth, eager for her caresses and treats. In the vision, Beth turned to him, laughing and smiling as she called out the horse's name. "Dakar says you've been neglecting him," she said in a teasing voice that made Omar realize that the horse's neglect was due to the attention he'd been giving Beth.

The tent flap opened again and a young girl stepped into the sunlight. Her hair was mahogany brown, and her features were his....

"Omar?" Beth whispered, her hand touching his cheek, pulling him back from the vision. "Is something wrong?"

"Something is either very wrong or very right," he said, aware that his voice was rough with emotion. He didn't understand the dream. Was it a glimpse of the future or a warning?

Beth's hands turned his face back to hers. "Tell me about it," she said.

Instead, he bent and kissed her. As their mouths connected and he felt her willingness, everything else disappeared from his mind.

Dream or nightmare, he couldn't say what he'd witnessed. For all that he was the descendant of Con, he'd never had prophetic abilities.

He didn't care, either. All that mattered was Beth.

His hand moved beneath her robe, sliding up her thigh. He marveled again at the strength of her slender body. Many years ago he'd accepted the duties of his people. As he bent to untie Beth's robe, he accepted that he was a man possessed.

BETH KNEW she was revealing all her need of Omar as she pulled him to her and kissed him without restraint. It was insane. Completely and totally without reason or caution. With that in mind she kissed him more deeply, until there was no going back to reason. There was only Omar, his touch igniting her body and creating needs she'd never known.

She'd been asleep, deeply, and something about that worried her. It didn't matter now, though. All that mattered was this moment. She would have this man she loved one more time, no matter the cost.

Chapter Fourteen

As he rose from the bed of pillows, Omar felt Beth grip his leg, gently holding him in place.

"Where are you going?" she asked.

"I've been away for too long. I have business that must be taken care of." He rumpled her hair. "Finish your rest. You remind me of a princess when you're asleep."

"She drugged me," Beth said, rolling onto an elbow.

"I know. She won't do it again."

Beth's smile was lazy with satisfaction. To hear Omar admit to the truth made her drop the last barrier to trusting him. "First of all, I never dreamed anyone would slip me a Mickey—isn't that what they call it in detective novels?" She rushed on. "Secondly, I never thought I could be so casual about it. Why did she do it?"

Omar stood taller, but it was something Beth didn't miss. She was learning to read this man. Whenever he assumed the burden of leadership for his people, his posture reflected it.

"She thought she was helping me," he said. "She

knew I wanted to keep you safe. She wasn't certain you would heed my warnings. So she took matters into her own hands and made sure you were…compliant.''

"Like all the other women of your tribe," Beth teased.

Omar laughed. "If only that were true. My people obey my rule, but they aren't compliant. No desert people bend easily."

"So I'm learning," Beth said. Her fingers trailed slowly up his leg. "I'm learning a lot of things."

He caught her hand and knelt beside her. With great deliberation, he brought her hand to his lips. He kissed the fingertips, the palm, the wrist. At each spot, Beth felt her skin begin to tingle and burn. His touch was like a wildfire that roared through her, burning away all inhibitions and all other concerns. Once she would have been frightened of such a conflagration. Now she yearned for it.

"You're going to tax my stamina," Omar whispered into her ear, his lips nibbling and his tongue teasing.

"I doubt that," Beth murmured.

He pulled away from her. "I would spend the rest of the night with you if I could," he said. "The rest of the week. The rest of…" He remembered the vision and let the sentence fade away.

"I have to go back to Alexandria. Mauve, John…" She shrugged. "I'm not a leader like you, but these people put their trust in me and followed me here."

"And then they betrayed you."

"Not all of them," Beth said. "Only three of them. I fired them and left their return air tickets with John." She couldn't help a lopsided smile. "And their passports. I was mad enough at the time that I thought it would be their just reward if I made it difficult for them to get home."

"Exactly what they deserve," Omar said.

"I know, but I can't do that. I'll give them their papers and tickets home. I just don't want them around anymore."

"And John?"

"I don't know," she admitted. "He wasn't in on the betrayal. Or maybe he just didn't have the opportunity to join. Ray and Judy find him as annoying as I do."

Omar's smile was understanding. "I know. John is a man who can try the patience of the sand."

"At any rate, I have to get back tomorrow." She had decided to retain Omar as her guide. She'd have to cancel her appointment with the other man.

He nodded. "I'll see that you're there."

"What would *you* do about John?" she asked.

"My personal dislike for the man is intense. I can't evaluate his usefulness to your trip. If I could do without him, I would."

"There's the rub," Beth said. "If I let Judy, Sam and Ray go, I need John."

"Then you have your answer."

Beth leaned back against the pillows. Having Omar beside her, talking with her, offering advice but not pressing her to take it, was something she'd never anticipated. She'd longed to have someone to share her life with. This was only a passing moment, but she gave herself permission to enjoy it fully.

"I could forgive Ray and Judy and Sam," she said, testing the idea out loud.

"Could you?" Omar leaned toward her. His hands caught hers and held them. "Could you really forgive them?"

Beth was startled at the passion in his voice. "I don't know," she said. "Maybe. I understand being driven. I've been driven all my life. I just never wanted something badly enough to step on someone along the way."

"And you could forgive them for betraying you?"

"Attempted betrayal," she said, putting her palm against his flushed cheek. "In my country, the law differentiates between an attempt and a successful completion of the act."

"In my country, it is understood that the act is committed in the heart long before the hand carries it through. We are not so lenient."

"I know." Beth nodded. "I'd have to listen to their side. People aren't always clear about their motives. They act before they think things through."

"Your heart is big," Omar said. "You have the traits of a leader."

"Is that why you put up with Keya? Because you can forgive her?"

The look on Omar's face told her she was right on target. "I suppose that's so," he said "I've never thought it through. If it weren't for me, she would be the leader of our people. I can see where she both loves me and hates me."

Beth nodded. "Conflicting emotions, conflicting needs. Life would be so much simpler if there was only one way to feel about things."

"You are brilliant," Omar said, bending to kiss her

cheek. He rose abruptly. "I'll have food brought to you."

"I'd like to walk around the settlement."

Omar's hesitation was very brief, but Beth saw it. Was it that he didn't trust her? Or Keya?

"I'll get Yemal to accompany you." He cut her protest short. "He speaks fluent English. He can interpret for you."

"Thank you, Omar," she said, yielding gracefully to the arrangement. Yemal was young and eager to please. He wouldn't be as big an impediment as some other guard. Beth had no objection to Omar's regard for her safety, but she didn't like the idea of being guarded as if she were a national treasure or a potential felon. But these were all things that would take care of themselves.

"Will you come back here tonight? To sleep with me?" she asked Omar. "I'd like that."

"Your reputation is already ruined in the settlement. Intimacy before marriage can mark a woman for life."

He was jesting, and Beth laughed. "I'll risk it."

"Then I'll return to you," he said. "While you're lost in your dreams, I'll slip in beside you and hold you in my arms. Perhaps you can take me to the places you travel in your sleep."

"Perhaps," she said, barely able to swallow. There were times Omar said things that were almost too perceptive.

Omar kissed her once more and then rose. "I'll be back as soon as I can."

"Omar, tell me the truth. You're going after your horses, aren't you?" Beth tried not to show her fear.

Omar reached out and touched her cheek. "I have two choices. I can offer you the comfort of a lie or tell the truth."

Beth saw that he was offering her the choice.

"The truth, Omar. Always. You can't protect me with lies." Judging from the glow in his eyes, her words had touched something deep inside him.

"Night has fallen. If I don't act soon, the horses will be sent far away."

It was the truth, unvarnished, exactly as she had asked, and it made her heart lurch with fear. "Let me go with you."

He shook his head. "No, Beth. I'm not looking for trouble, but should it come, I would be at a disadvantage if I were worried for your safety."

"Yet I must sit here and worry about yours," she countered.

"You must trust me to take care of myself."

"Trust must work both ways, Omar."

"I do trust you, Beth. I trust your heart and your words. I trust your intelligence. But you haven't been trained to fight. I have. The men who will go with me have, also."

Beth sighed. "Be careful, Omar."

"You have my word on that."

Beth sat among the pillows and watched him leave. When he swept open the flap of the tent, she saw a million stars in a black-velvet sky.

OMAR STOPPED long enough to speak with Yemal. He explained Beth's wish to explore the settlement and asked the young man to accompany her. He saw

Yemal's bitter disappointment at not being chosen for the raid to retrieve the horses.

"As much as I value my horses, I value Beth more," Omar said, putting a hand on the young man's shoulder. "Guard her with your life, Yemal. I've entrusted you with a far greater mission. And I'm leaving Kaf in your care. You'll help Keya with the breeding program if I don't return."

"Of course," Yemal answered, biting at his bottom lip.

"If I'm not back by dawn, you are to gather the most experienced men and come looking for us."

"And the woman?"

"If I haven't returned by morning, Beth has far more to worry about than being left here with Keya. My cousin will see to her safe return to Alexandria."

"Your wishes will be carried out," Yemal said.

Omar squeezed Yemal's shoulder before heading toward the horses that were saddled and waiting. He'd chosen his men with great care. All were expert horsemen and all were skilled in the use of a knife. They had guns, but this was a time for silence. The traditional weapon of the nomad was his choice.

His men were waiting for him, and one held the reins of a prancing bay gelding. Zetta was both fast and intelligent, and he was also strong-willed. He was the perfect mount for the ride ahead.

"I believe the horses are in the Cemen stronghold," Omar told the men. "We will bring them home without bloodshed, if at all possible."

"And we will also punish the thieves?" one man asked.

"Only if there's no other way," Omar said.

"If we don't show them that there's a penalty for stealing from us, they will return and do it again."

"Justice is a difficult mistress," Omar said. He understood the man's desire for revenge. Mica had been one of the men beaten in his attempt to prevent the theft. "We serve her best sometimes by waiting for the right moment to strike."

Mica thought a moment before he nodded agreement. "But we *will* strike back at them?"

"Once we learn what was behind the theft." Omar decided to tell the men what he was thinking. "Our horses weren't taken simply because they are fine horses. This raid had another purpose."

"What would that be?" Mica asked.

"A warning to me, perhaps. Or a distraction. I'm not certain. But I want to get our horses and bring them home. If we can do this without calling attention to ourselves, we're ahead of the game."

The men were in accord. Now it was time for action. He glanced only once at the tent where Beth was, but he saw, in the dark night, their smiles of amusement. Some of them had been married for years. Others were young, single men. But all of them had waited for him to find the woman who would stand by his side.

If only it could be Beth.

But that was a hurdle to jump another day. The first priority was the horses.

BETH WAITED until she heard the horsemen leave the settlement. Although the blue robe was extremely modest, she felt naked wearing it. The material whispered over her highly sensitized skin, reminding her of Omar's lightest touch.

There was nothing else to wear, though. She'd brought nothing except the small leather pouch, and she pulled it from beneath several pillows. Opening it carefully, she made sure that all the images of the hieroglyphics Mauve had printed out were still there. All was just as she'd left it, and she returned the pouch to the hiding place.

Stepping to the tent flap, she saw Yemal. He was crouched before a small fire, eating halfheartedly from a platter of food. As soon as she touched the opening of the tent, though, he was on his feet and headed her way.

"Omar said I could walk around and explore the settlement," she said with a smile. "He said you would be my guide and interpreter."

"Yes." Yemal tried hard, but disappointment was evident in his voice.

"Tell me about this oasis," Beth requested as she stepped into the night. The temperature had dropped at least twenty degrees. She was astounded.

"It is the Oasis Lusha. We're about thirty miles south of Alexandria and some fifteen miles from the Nile River."

"Omar said this isn't a popular oasis."

"Not for tourists or long-distance travelers. It's too close to Alexandria. Most caravans head for one of the bigger oases farther away. The trick to desert travel is to go as far as possible each day, ending in a place where the animals can drink and rest."

"So this is your own private oasis?" Beth asked. Her question seemed to make him uncomfortable.

"The oasis belongs to no one," Yemal said. "We share it."

"But if no one else…" Beth decided to let the subject drop. "Tell me about your people."

"There is little to tell. We are nomads. Omar is developing a line of horses that will one day give all our descendants a comfortable way of life."

"He's a very smart man," Beth said.

Yemal dared to look her directly in the eyes. "Will you marry him?"

"He hasn't asked." Beth took the guide's elbow and began to move him away from her tent.

"If he does?"

"What would your people think of that?" Beth almost couldn't ask the question. She was afraid of the answer. What if Yemal said the tribe would not understand?

"There are those who would be upset, but Omar is the leader. He can do as he chooses."

"Even when it comes to marrying an American woman?"

"He is the ruler. His word is law."

"But would he lose respect?"

"You have asked a good question," Yemal said. "Do you care?"

"Of course I would care," Beth said. "If Omar lost the respect of his people, he would never be able to respect himself. He would be miserable."

Yemal grinned. "You know him well."

"That part isn't hard to know," Beth said. "What

about the women here? Surely there's one he might marry.''

"He could have his pick, but he doesn't pursue any of them." Yemal shrugged. "Omar is an old man, but he hasn't taken a wife. I'm only eighteen, and this summer I will wed."

"Omar isn't old," Beth said. "He's only, what, thirty-five?"

"That is old in our culture."

"Then I must be old, too." Beth laughed. "I'm thirty-two."

"If you were a pharaoh, someone would be building a tomb for you right this minute."

Beth laughed in delight. Yemal was young, but he was accomplished in language and easy wit. "Show me the horses," she requested.

They walked through the settlement, stopping so that Beth could look at the horses and camels. She found her little bay mare easily, and the horse gave a low whinny of greeting.

"She remembers you," Yemal said. "Arabians are very intelligent, and Leah is one of the smartest."

Beth noted that the mare was on the far side of the settlement. Beyond her was only the darkened desert. A plan had been forming in her mind ever since Omar had confessed that he was going on a raid to retrieve his stolen horses. He didn't want her to go, but she was damned if she was going to stay behind. Omar had tried to make it sound as if the man who'd stolen his horses would simply give them back. She wasn't naive enough to believe that.

"You said the next oasis is due south of here?" She

looked up at the night sky, pinpointing the constellations that would guide her across the desert. "How far away?"

"A good distance. Twenty miles at least."

"What about the tribe of Cemen that Omar was talking about? Are they nomads, too?"

"Yes, we were once very close. We often camped in the same oasis. That was when Omar's mother was our leader. I think Jordel, the leader of the Cemen, wanted to marry Aleta." He grinned. "She wouldn't consider marrying anyone. She had her sons and her people."

Beth pointed to one of the camels and led Yemal in that direction. He explained how camels were trained. As he continued to walk and talk with Beth, she could see that he was letting his guard down.

"What happened to Omar's father?" she asked when they had circled the perimeter of the encampment.

"What do you mean?"

"How did he die?" she asked.

Yemal gave her a curious look. "He isn't dead. He lives in Cairo."

"But I thought…" She realized she'd assumed Suleman Dukhan had died. "He just left his wife and two sons?"

"It is difficult for a man to live in the shadow of his wife."

"He wasn't from your people, was he."

"No, he was a scientist who came into the desert. Aleta met him and married him against the wishes of her mother. He was never happy in the desert. Finally he left, but the price he paid was to give up his sons.''

''Does Omar ever see him?''

Yemal shrugged. ''That's a question you need to ask him, not me. Now you should go back to your tent. It's late.''

''When will Omar return?''

She saw the worry in Yemal's eyes. ''When he has our horses and not before.''

''Is he in danger?'' Beth couldn't help herself. Yemal's worry was contagious.

''The tribe of Cemen are strong fighters. We have never been enemies before this time. It will be a hard fight.''

''Where are they?'' Beth asked, her hand lightly grasping Yemal's arm. ''Tell me.''

''I can't,'' he said, turning away. ''Omar will come to you when he returns. You must wait for him, just as I do. Instead, I will tell you of a secret place. It was designed as a tomb, but then was used for a very different purpose.''

Beth was intrigued, despite herself. ''What purpose is that?''

''Omar will tell you all of it when he returns. It is the place he wants you to see. I will tell you only enough to make you anxious to see it and to distract you from worrying about Omar.''

''Tell me,'' Beth said.

''It was designed for a very special ruler. At first it was going to be a tomb, but that was not to be. This ruler grew in popularity and power, until another burial site was created.''

"Who was the ruler?" Beth asked, trying hard to fit the tiny bits of real information Yemal was giving her into some historical context.

"Omar will tell you," Yemal said, a frown creasing his forehead. "It is his secret to share."

They were at her tent and Yemal held open the flap. It was obvious he intended her to go inside and do as Omar had bidden her. "Then I shall have to wait for him to tell me," she said.

"A wise woman would do exactly that," Yemal said with a hint of relief.

Chapter Fifteen

Omar crept to the top of the sand dune. He anticipated seeing the settlement of the Cemen tribe on the opposite side of the dune. The nomadic tribes often sought brief rest in the lee of a dune.

Omar and his men had ridden long and hard, and now all their stealth and skill as desert men would be required. His plan was to slip into the settlement, select his horses and leave—without a confrontation, if at all possible.

Though several of the men wanted to shed blood, he had convinced them otherwise. Judgment and revenge would come later. Getting the horses was top priority. He would deal with the Cemens in his own time. That was the art of revenge—selecting the most effective and the least costly time and place to administer it.

He made it to the top of the dune and looked back at his men. They were all loyal and brave. He would trust his life to any of them.

A few more steps and he was able to see over the dune. He inhaled sharply. Except for the twelve horses staked in the sand, there wasn't any sign of a settlement. It was as if the tribe of Cemen had been swallowed by the earth.

He stood and signaled his men to come up to him. "We've been tricked," one of them said as soon as he saw the horses. "We've been lured out here. Why?"

"To leave our settlement unprotected," Omar said. "They stole the horses to get us to chase after them. Now they are where we should be."

"Why?" Mica cried. "What have we done to the Cemen? They were once our brothers. Why would they do this to us?"

"A better question is what do they want," Omar said. "Gather the horses and change your mounts. We ride back as fast as possible."

No matter how fast they rode, Omar knew they would be too late. Whatever plan was afoot, he was at least two hours away from being able to protect his people—and Beth.

He felt as if cold water had splashed over his spine. Beth. That was what this was all about. It didn't make any sense, but somehow, she was at the center of the horse theft.

She was in grave danger.

He urged his horse down the dune. In a moment he'd unsaddled the gelding and saddled a fresh mount. Using a long rope, he tethered three of the riderless horses together. His men had done the same.

"Ride," he said tersely.

They set out at a gallop, the sand kicked up by the horses' hooves flying silver in the moonlight as they rode toward home.

BETH HAD ALMOST convinced herself to accept her confinement with grace when she heard what sounded like vehicles approaching. She'd been studying the images of the hieroglyphics, trying to find some way to decipher them. Carefully she put the images back inside the leather pouch and stood. All her senses became attuned to what was happening outside her tent. She went to the flap and inched it open. Yemal, too, had risen to his feet and was listening attentively to something in the distance.

She was completely unprepared when a loud, vocal trill broke across the night. The sound was picked up by others, an effective warning system. Beth knew what was happening. The raiders had returned. The men who'd stolen Omar's horses had come back.

She'd never attempted to break out of a tent, and she was surprised to discover that the bottom was buried deep in the sand. It took a lot more work than she'd imagined to dig out the back of the tent. At last she'd made a furrow deep enough to slip under. She pushed the pouch containing the photographs ahead of her. Once she was clear of the tent, she didn't waste a second.

In her stroll with Yemal, she'd found out exactly where Leah was and where to locate a saddle. She had also learned the direction in which she should head. She had water and some food—not enough to survive on for days, but plenty to keep her strength up until she found Omar. She had to let him know what was happening with his people.

Heading due south, she could miss Omar by miles. But she had to try. As she slipped from shadow to shadow, she cursed the full moon. It seemed to burn a thousand times brighter over the sand. If she wasn't a scientist, she'd have been easily able to imagine lost caravans walking the tops of the dunes in the distance. Ghost caravans, those unlucky explorers and merchants who'd gone astray on the ever-shifting sand. Lucky for her, she *was* a scientist.

Leah greeted her with a soft whinny. It took Beth only a few minutes to saddle the mare and mount. If she was going to be caught, now would be the time. Hoping that no one would see her, Beth walked the mare out of the camp and into the desert. It was only when she was well clear of the settlement that she turned south and urged the mare into a gallop. When she thought she was a safe distance away, she stopped and twisted around to see behind her.

The glare of headlights seemed to ring the settlement. One, two, three—Beth counted six vehicles. Adrenaline rushed through her. Her gut instinct told her to run as hard and fast in the opposite direction as the could go. Instead, she soothed the dancing, excited Leah, torn by conflicting emotions.

Gunshots echoed in the night, and flames leaped from one of the tents. In the glow of the fire she could see women and children running in every direction. Several men with automatic weapons were silhouetted by the fire.

Fists clenched, Beth was helpless to stop what was happening. She turned Leah south, then squeezing the mare's ribs with her legs, she took the willing animal into another gallop. Then she remembered that Omar had left Kaf in the settlement. Instead of riding the stallion, he'd left him to rest.

Beth pulled Leah to a halt. She knew what was happening. The horse thieves had come back for Kaf.

"We have to get him," she said to Leah.

The little mare pranced beneath her, pulling at the reins in her desire to go.

Beth knew where the stallion was—right outside her tent. Yemal would guard him with his life, but the men in the military transports had superior firepower. The battle was badly mismatched.

About a hundred yards from the oasis, Beth slid from Leah's back. She dropped the reins to the ground in the way Omar had taught her to ground-tie a horse. She made sure her pouch was still tied to Leah's saddle. Of all of her possessions, the images that showed the way to Con's lost city were the most valuable thing she owned. Still, she had to leave them behind and trust that she would return to reclaim them.

Another volley of shots split the desert night. She was close enough to hear the men in military uniforms shouting orders and the crying and screaming of the women. Several tents were burning. It was a scene from hell, and Beth wanted only to turn and run back into the safety of the night.

Swallowing the fear that threatened to paralyze her, Beth crept toward the camp. Kaf was the promise of the future for Omar. She couldn't stop the invaders, but she might be able to rescue the stallion.

The closer Beth crept to the camp, the more confused she became. The men who had invaded were in some kind of uniform. They weren't members of Egypt's army, but some private mercenary group.

Two of the men were talking with Keya. She was gesturing wildly toward the west. The men shook their heads in disbelief, then one of them slapped her.

Keya looked stunned. Two more men brought Yemal up to the group. His hands were tied behind his back and he was bleeding. When they asked him a question, he spat at them.

Beth turned her head when one of the men punched him in the face with the butt of a rifle.

"Kaf," she whispered. She had to get the stallion. And she couldn't afford to get caught.

Skirting the settlement, she saw that the men had already recognized Kaf. He was tethered to the back of one of the military trucks pawing with his front foot as if he knew that his people were in grave danger.

It was ironic that the attackers had made it easier for Beth by tying Kaf to the truck and leaving him alone. He was on the outskirts of the settlement.

Beth inched toward the truck. When she reached the side of it, she exhaled, then drew in a long breath. "Kaf," she whispered.

The stallion quit pawing and perked his ears forward, listening.

"I'm here. Be good now. I have to do something first." Beth was surprised that no one was guarding the vehicles. The invaders were all in the settlement.

Her work had often taken her to desolate locations. Survival had required that she learn the basics of motor mechanics. Slipping in the driver's door, she popped the hood, then went back out and lifted the hood only a few inches. She slid her arm inside and groped around for the spark-plug harness. When her fingers finally grasped it, she tugged with all her might. The entire harness came out in her hand.

One down, five to go, she thought as she moved to the next.

She'd disabled three of the vehicles when she realized she didn't have time to work on the others. With the harnesses still in her hand, she went to Kaf. He pushed his nose into her chest, almost knocking her down.

There was no time for a saddle and Beth had no confidence that she could stay on his back without one, but there wasn't time to hesitate. She untied him and swung up onto his back.

Kaf shot out of the settlement like an arrow. Swift and true, he flew over the sand, attentive to Beth's slightest weight shift on his back. It seemed that whenever she lost her balance and began to slip to one side, Kaf moved under her, picking her up without even breaking his stride.

Riding during the day had been exhilarating. Riding at night was magical. Beth gently guided Kaf to where she'd left Leah.

Before they got there, she heard a soft whinny. Leah recognized Kaf and was calling to him, guiding them both to her.

Kaf swung by the mare, hardly even slowing. Still, Beth was able to scoop up Leah's reins, and Leah fell into step at Kaf's hip. Together the three of them flew over the desert, Beth hoping against hope that they would somehow intersect with Omar.

IT'S MIDNIGHT in the exotic city of Alexandria, and still no sign of Miss Explorer. Somehow I don't think a *horseback ride should last longer than a few hours. So what gives? Has Omar kidnapped Beth?*

I have to admit, I'm worried. So is Mauve. She's been pacing the lobby of the hotel like a prisoner. John, too, has disappeared. His bags are in his room, though. Ray, Judy and Sam packed their bags earlier. I can only assume that they are headed back to the States.

Frankly, my dear, I don't give a hoot what happens to the traitors, but I should never have let Beth go off alone with Omar. I should have thought it through a little better and realized that it wasn't a good idea.

Sometimes it's difficult to find a horse willing to take a feline for a ride, for cats are predators. Once, a long, long time ago, my grandparents used to eat their grandparents. My grandparents used the old "cat in a tree" trick. They would hide in the tree limbs, generally beside a stream, and wait for a horse to come along and stand in the shade to drink water. Then they would jump out of the tree onto the horse's back. From that position, they could gain access to the horse's throat. The horse was lunch.

It seems that horses have very, very long genetic memories. They really don't want a cat on their back. Not even a domestic cat with his own PI license.

Still, I should have pressed the issue. But who would have thought Beth would simply leave and not return? Every day that her crew and equipment stand idle, that's money burned. She knows this. So where is she?

I can only deduce that something bad has happened. I suppose I'll have to figure out where she's gone and *then devise a plan to get there. Mauve will be my ticket to the desert. If I can only make her understand that she needs to hire horses and a guide.*

She's pretty smart for a humanoid. And she sincerely views Beth as a friend. I guess the best way to begin is with what passes for the Egyptian yellow pages. There are bound to be stables listed. We'll just take it one step at a time. I have until morning to make Mauve realize that Beth has vanished into the desert with Omar.

Time is the enemy, though. I feel like time is running out for Beth and Omar. Some folks would call it superstition, but we cats know that it's intuition. I better kick up a little dust and get moving.

OMAR RODE HARD, and the ride was made longer by the dread that seemed to weigh him down. He'd been lured away from his people like a fool. He'd done exactly as his enemy had wished, leaving his settlement open to attack.

But who was his enemy, and what did they want?

Omar wasn't naive enough to believe that he didn't have enemies. No man or woman who ruled escaped without earning the enmity of some.

The question that nagged at him was the timing of these attacks. Why now? Why had the Cemen people stolen his horses at this particular time? The two tribes had bartered and traded together for generations. Jordel, the leader of the Cemens, had once wished to wed his mother. Aleta had refused, and that refusal had infuriated Jordel. That was years ago, though. That was long buried beneath the sands of the desert.

Beth was the newest element in his life, and one attempt had already been made on her life. Someone had tried to kill her with an ancient poison, one that most modern doctors would never have recognized. Had he not seen the symptoms, Mauve would have died.

It was only since his association with Beth that his people had been attacked. And she was at the camp now, where he was positive another assault was being led against his people.

Beth was there, and so was Kaf. Two of the most important things in the world to him.

His intensity communicated itself to his horse, and though the mare was tired, she strained forward, lengthening her stride and gobbling the miles beneath her flying hooves.

He and his men could ride no faster. The valiant horses were already giving everything they had. To continue to press the animals would lead only to a long rest period—or the horses' deaths. He gave the signal to slow.

In the moonlight, he saw the desperation on the faces of his men. They knew what was likely happening back in the settlement. Many, many years had passed since one tribe had deliberately attacked another. Now it was happening again, and it was always the women and children who suffered the most.

"Whatever we find," he said, trying to force back the images of Beth and his people that rushed into his mind, "we must not lose our self-control." He wondered if he spoke for his own benefit more than that of his men.

"If they've harmed our women and children, they will die," one of the men said in a tone that brooked no disagreement.

"Yes," Omar agreed. But even as he spoke, he knew that no amount of bloodshed would undo the damage to his heart if Beth was injured or dead. No amount of revenge would compensate for the pain and suffering of his people.

"How much farther?" a man asked.

"An hour," Omar answered, knowing it would be the longest hour of his life.

Chapter Sixteen

Mauve is frantic with worry. She's discovered that the prints she made of the hieroglyphics are gone. Along with Beth. Even worse, Mauve doesn't know whom to trust and she isn't inclined to pay much attention to me. Unlike Beth, she can't accept that I'm trying to help her. She's pacing the floor as if she has hot pepper in her shoes.

She's headed for Beth's room. I'll follow. She's searching through Beth's things, trying to figure out how much our Miss Explorer took with her. And she's coming quickly to the conclusion that Beth didn't intend to be gone overnight. None of her personal items are missing.

Someone's knocking at the door. John Gilmore. And Mauve is so worried that even John can see it. He looks worried, too, but I can't help but wonder why. Is he concerned for Beth or afraid she's left him behind?

He's sending Mauve down to the desk to see if Beth left a message for anyone. He's checking his watch and looking at the telephone, which is ringing.

He's picked up the phone, but he's not saying a word. He's merely listening.

Then he says, "Yes, I'll take care of it."

And he hangs up the phone and leaves without a backward glance. What I wouldn't give to know who was on the other end of the line.

I don't trust John any further than I can trust the other crew members. All of them, except Mauve, are capable of the worst type of betrayal. That's why I'm getting Mauve organized and out of here.

I'll slip over to her room and get the disk with all the hieroglyphics on it. We can't leave that behind for prying eyes. Now, let me pull some jeans and boots out of her closet. A jacket for the cold night air. We're desert bound, and no one is going to stop us.

Here's Mauve. I can tell by the expression on her face that there wasn't a note from Beth. We can't wait around any longer. We're going to have to try to track her down.

I just have to make Mauve realize she has to change clothes and follow me. She's looking at the clothing I selected as if it was a space suit. But she's picking the items up and thinking about them. Eureka! She's putting them on and tucking the disk into her pocket.

Now we're headed down to the lobby. And who should be standing there but the other Dukhan. Harad. He's asking about Beth and Omar.

Mauve is smitten by Harad's good looks, but she also has sense enough to keep her lip zipped. She isn't telling Harad anything, except that Beth and Omar aren't here and that Beth was wearing jeans and boots when she left.

Harad is telling her about a stable at the edge of town. Omar keeps horses there. He's telling her to check and see. If Omar's stallion is missing, then chances are good that he took Beth for a ride in the desert. But Harad's forehead is furrowed. He's worried, too. He's going to send a guide to meet us at the stable.

This is good—unless it's just another trick. I'm not sure we can trust Harad, but we don't really have another option.

Harad has left, and Mauve is putting a call through to the States. She's calling Beth's sister, Amelia. There's no answer! Dang! But Mauve is leaving a message. She's urging Amelia to come to Alexandria. She's saying that Beth has been kidnapped by a desert sheik! She's telling Amelia about the poison and the betrayals. Good. At least we've left a trail of bread crumbs. Now it's hi-ho Silver and away.

BETH HAD SLOWED Kaf from a gallop to a trot and now to a walk. He seemed none the worse for wear, but she was exhausted. Once she was away from the settlement, she'd stopped long enough to transfer the saddle from Leah to Kaf. The stallion could continue all night—his stamina was incredible.

The problem was, Beth had begun to worry that she was lost. She'd been judging her course by the constellations that she knew, but with each passing minute, she felt her confidence wavering.

The desert was vast. No matter what direction she looked, there was only sand and more sand. And once daylight arrived, she'd soon be sweltering under the sun. If she was truly lost in the desert, she and the horses would quickly die of thirst.

It was nearly four in the morning, and there was no sign of Omar. She'd traveled for nearly five hours. By now she should have crossed his path.

Beneath concerns for her own survival were worries about Omar's people. What had happened to the settlement?

She clenched her jaw and tried not to think about it. Once, while working in the Arizona desert, she'd unearthed the site of a massacre. Indian women and children had died standing in a line beside a wall. Mothers had died with infants in their arms, younger children clinging to their legs.

The bones had left no clues about why they'd been killed or who had killed them. Time had erased such knowledge. But the horror of that kind of death was never far from Beth's mind. The same thing could have happened in Omar's village.

Everyone she'd talked to earlier in the day might now be dead. Thinking of that, she berated herself. She should have stayed and fought. She had saved Kaf, but it wasn't nearly enough.

"Omar!" she called as loudly as she could. To hope he might hear her and answer was a fool's dream, but it was the only thing she had left to cling to.

"Omar!" His name seemed to echo across the sand and disappear in the black silence.

Tired and sick with fear, she gave Kaf his head and let him wander through the sand. Perhaps the horse had a better sense of direction than she did. It couldn't hurt to try.

OMAR SMELLED the fire before he saw the settlement. The men smelled it, too, and fear of what they might

find registered on their faces as they urged their tired
horses over the last dune.

Several fires were still burning, and against the
flames Omar could see people moving. Three military
vehicles had been abandoned near the perimeter of the
settlement. He rode forward, fighting back both rage
and worry.

"Omar!"

He heard his cousin call his name, and he leaped
from the horse and ran to her. She was standing beside
his burning tent, and he saw that one side of her face
was cut and swollen.

"What happened?" He grasped her arms and held
her. "Where's Beth?"

Keya's dark eyes narrowed. "Kaf is gone, and so is
the woman."

"Where?"

She shrugged free of his grip. "The men came and
started burning the tents. Yemal and I both tried to find
the woman. She was gone. Perhaps she left with them
voluntarily."

"I doubt that," Omar said angrily. "And Kaf? What
happened to him?"

"They had him tied to the back of a truck. Then he
was gone." Her smile was victorious. "Someone took
him away. The men were furious. They'd come for the
woman and the horse and they didn't get Kaf."

"How do you know they came for Kaf and Beth?"

Keya's mouth hardened. "They asked for the
woman. They knew her name. They searched the set-

tlement for her before they began to set fires and injure people."

"How can you think she left with them voluntarily?" Omar asked, still angry. "They came to kidnap her."

"Perhaps she gave them the signal to come."

"Where is Yemal?" Omar demanded.

"Tending to his younger brother. He was injured." Keya's hand gripped Omar's forearm. "Several others were injured. Your concern for them is touching. The woman is the only thing you care about."

"Keya, you go too far."

"No, Omar, it's you who go too far. You put that woman ahead of everything else. If you can't put your people first, then you should step down as our leader."

"And give the reins of power to you?"

"I am next in line."

"What is it that you would do so differently from me?" Omar asked. His cousin burned with ambition, and for the first time he realized that time would never heal her lust for the position he held.

She could barely contain her bitterness as she spoke. "With only one other exception, the people of Con have always been led by a woman. Your father was not of the people. He has tainted you with an interest in Western things. Like your brother, you hunger for things our people do not need."

"Like Beth?" he asked pointedly.

"Like the woman," Keya agreed. "You spend half your time in the cities when you should be here with your people."

"I've been trying to develop a horse-breeding program, Keya, so that our people can survive. The days of caravans are quickly coming to an end.''

"You see the end of our ways because that is what suits you."

Omar sighed. This was an old argument, and one he wasn't going to win.

"We both see what suits us," Omar said almost sadly. "The difference is that I see a way to help our people survive in a changing world. I may not like it, but I know that it is coming. You see only the past and a road that will lead to complete destruction of this tribe. If I ever had an inclination to step aside and let you rule, I understand now that I would be dooming our people to extinction.''

Keya stepped back from him. "Your arrogance only exceeds your stupidity." She whirled and stormed away.

Omar's concern for Keya faded the moment she was gone. She would grow older and more bitter with each passing year. It was her destiny. His concern now was Beth, his people and Kaf.

He walked through the settlement, taking in the weariness and shock his people showed. The horror of the attack was fading. Dealing with the reality would be the next step. He understood that such an attack could erode the foundation of peace and safety that was so necessary for survival. He would punish the men who had stolen this. Once he found Beth and Kaf, he would see that the debt was paid.

He found Yemal kneeling beside a young man in his early teens. The boy had a head wound and minor burns on his hands and arms. The right side of Yemal's face was swollen and bruised.

"How is he?" Omar asked, kneeling beside Yemal and Yosef. "How are you?"

"My pride is hurt, and my brother is going to be okay." Yemal finally looked up at Omar. "I failed you. The woman is gone."

"Is there a chance she escaped the men?" Omar kept his question gentle. Yemal already suffered too much.

"I don't know. The men came and began searching for her. She'd slipped out the back. They set fire to the tent. They went through all the things in the tent. They were looking for Beth, and for something else, too."

"What?"

"I don't know. They didn't say. They were just angry that they couldn't find it. That's when they began hitting us and setting things on fire. They said we would tell them or they would destroy the settlement and kill all the horses. Even Kaf."

"They had Kaf tied to a truck," Omar prodded.

"Yes. They knew how valuable he was. I overheard them talking. They had forged papers for him and a buyer in America."

Omar felt his blood freeze. "A buyer in America? You're sure of that?"

"They said it," Yemal replied. "Does that help?"

"I don't know. Did they say anything else?"

"Only that they would find Beth and the thing she carried with her."

"Where is Leah?" Omar asked, remembering the little mare Beth had ridden to the settlement.

"She was gone, too. And a saddle."

"Beth got away! She left on horseback, across the desert." Omar felt a rush of hope. "Think hard, Yemal. Did she give any clues as to where she might be heading?"

Yemal's eyes widened. "She asked where I thought you had gone. She asked the direction. Then she talked about the stars."

Omar rose swiftly. "She went looking for me," he said. "She's out on the desert alone."

"Not alone, Omar. Those men are hunting her," Yemal reminded him.

REPLACING THE CANTEEN on her saddle horn, Beth knew she was in very serious trouble. There was only half a canteen left. The sun was just peaking over the horizon. Instead of relief, she felt despair. All around her the sand dunes rose and fell. She was more alone than she'd ever been in her entire life.

Judging by the sun, she realized she'd gone off course. She was headed due east. Somewhere, far in the distance, was the Nile River. How far she didn't have a clue. The probability that she and the horses could make it that far was very slim.

She stared into the sun as it slid free of the dunes. Ra was the sun god that the Egyptians worshiped. He was all powerful. The Egyptians had long understood that their survival depended on submitting to the unrelenting sun. She patted Kaf's neck and leaned forward in the saddle, resting on the horn and closing her eyes. It didn't really matter where they went. Instead of saving Kaf and Leah, she'd doomed them to a torturous death of thirst in the desert. Her fate was unavoidable. Now, though, she only wanted to sleep for a few minutes.

Beth felt the sun burning hot on her arms and face. When she opened her eyes again, she thought she was hallucinating. The square structure that seemed to rise out of the sand was crude, compared to the design and execution of the pyramids. The stone blocks were roughhewn, without the symmetrical finish of many Egyptian burial structures. And the design was strange. But it was shade, a place to rest out of the heat of the sun.

Checking her watch, Beth saw that it was only eight in the morning. Already she felt as if she were being roasted on a spit. Kaf, though he was only walking, was sweating. Leah, too. If they took shelter out of the sun and rested, they could last a little longer.

Kaf walked to the structure as if he knew the way. He entered the dark shadow of the opening with Leah close at his side. Once inside, he stopped.

Beth looked around in awe. While the outside of the structure was primitive and crude, the interior was simple elegance. A sundial in the center was carved with a likeness of Ra. It was a small building, supported by simple columns etched with the image of a feline and adorned with a climbing vine that looked familiar.

It took Beth a few moments to recognize the images as similar to the ones she'd discovered in the underwater temple built to worship Con.

Despite her fatigue, she felt a rush of anticipation. Slipping from Kaf's back, she walked deeper into the temple. What was it Omar had told her? There was a

burial site designed for a ruler, but it had never been
finished. The ruler had been buried elsewhere.

She heard something behind her and saw that Kaf
was nuzzling at a stone altar. Leah was at his side,
using her nose to push at the stone slab.

Curious, Beth went over to the horses. The stone slab
was at least four inches thick, but the horses seemed
determined to move it aside. As soon as she touched
the stone, Beth felt its coolness and put her back into
pushing it. When she couldn't budge the slab, she took
off the belt of her robe and tied it around an edge of
the slab. She tied the other end to Kaf's saddle. Then
she urged him forward with her voice, and inch by inch
it began to move.

The water beneath was cool and clear, and Beth felt
her throat convulse with the need for a drink.

"Walk," she called to Kaf. Only a few more inches
and the opening would be wide enough for the horses
to drink, too. "Walk."

Kaf leaned into the work and in a moment the slab
had shifted another few inches.

Beth untied the belt and led Kaf to the cistern. Leah
dipped her muzzle into the water and drank deeply.
Beth let them have several swallows before she backed
them off and drank herself.

Water! It was a miracle. They had nothing to eat,
but with the water they could last several days. In that
time, perhaps someone would come looking for them.

Perhaps.

It was a slim hope, but Beth knew that she would
cling to it as long as she could. Omar was a desert
man. Somehow, he would figure out where she was.

Chapter Seventeen

We left the stables at daybreak, and we've been traveling steadily ever since. I can tell you one thing, a black suit is not the best garb for a desert adventure. I'm about to die! Even Mauve is sweating. As are the horses.

All I can say is that it was only my keen intelligence that won me a ride up here behind Mauve. She didn't want me to go, but the guide was too superstitious to make me stay behind. Once I climbed up, he wasn't about to make me get down. His take on the situation was, if I wanted to go, I was welcome. Now I'm wondering how smart I really was. If we don't find some shade soon, I may swoon from the heat. The problem with that is, the guide may think I chose to swoon and just leave me behind. Being viewed as a god is a tricky situation.

I wish— Hey! Unless my eyes deceive me, I see green up ahead. I wonder if this is a mirage. I want green so desperately maybe I'm making it up. Who in the world would ever think that I, Familiar the Detective Cat, would lust for water? I want to lap it, jump in it, swim in it—I want it cascading down my sleek fur.

That oasis is no mirage. It's very real, and something bad has happened there. People are acting dazed or frantic. I smell fire, too. Tents have been burned! This settlement has been attacked! Mauve is about to leap out of the saddle. There's Omar, but there's no sign of Beth.

What in the world has happened? Omar is saddling another horse. Several men are also preparing for a ride.

I can't believe this. I just get here and it looks like it's going to be necessary for me to take another ride. First I have to figure out what happened. I'll follow Mauve.

MAUVE RAN TOWARD HIM and Omar knew that the worry on her face was a reflection of his own. He could also see the accusation in her eyes. It only intensified the guilt he already felt.

"Where's Beth?" Mauve demanded.

"We're searching for her. She disappeared from the camp last night." He watched Mauve's gaze sweep the settlement and take in the remains of burned tents and the many wounded, some of whom were reclining under the awning of another tent. None of the injuries were critical, but Omar recognized how awful the scene must look to Mauve.

"What happened?"

"Armed men attacked the settlement last night." Omar put a restraining hand on Mauve's arm. "Beth escaped before the attack. She was trying to find me, but she missed me."

"She's out there in the desert alone?" Mauve asked, her voice shaking. "How long?"

"Twelve hours," Omar admitted.

"How long can she last?"

"The rest of the day. Another night. Unless she finds water."

"There's no water in the desert," Mauve said. "We have to find her."

"We've been searching all morning," Omar told her. "We just came back for fresh horses and to see if she might have returned." His expression was rueful. "I've avoided modern conveniences all my life. I never thought that technology could improve my world, but I would give my right arm now for a cell phone and a call from Beth."

"Even if she had one, there aren't any towers," Mauve pointed out.

"Yes," Omar said, "you're right. But in a more modern world, finding Beth would not be the challenge it is." He looked out toward the desert and his expression was hopeless.

"What about helicopters? They could cover more ground."

Omar nodded. "My brother could arrange it. I've sent a messenger to Alexandria to ask him."

"He was worried about you," Mauve said. "I spoke with him before I left Alexandria. He helped me arrange to ride out here. Will he agree to help?"

Omar didn't hesitate. "Yes. He will do it instantly. But we must continue to search by land. We cannot give up. Beth is alive, I know it."

"You love her, don't you?" Mauve asked.

"Yes." Omar knew that to deny it would be to deny the only true thing he'd known in years. Now that she was gone, he saw clearly that nothing else mattered. Protecting the past—the job he had put ahead of all others—meant nothing without Beth in his life.

"I'm not much of a horsewoman, but I'll search, too."

"Good. We need everyone." Omar finally noticed the black cat at Mauve's feet. "So, you brought Familiar," he said.

"Familiar was coming whether I wanted him to or not," Mauve said. "He seems to be as attached to Beth as we are."

Omar stared at the cat. "He looks like he's had a rough morning."

"Riding horseback isn't his favorite mode of transportation," Mauve said. "He kept digging his claws into my hips to keep from falling off. This time he's riding with you."

Omar found a weak smile. "Drink some water, eat and rest a few moments. We'll head out again soon. We're gradually working to the southeast."

"What's out there?" Mauve asked.

"Sand," Omar answered. "Nothing but sand." In that answer was Beth's fate, unless they got to her first.

He took the reins from Mauve's hands and started to the small spring in the center of the oasis. It was difficult for him to look at the water, thinking that Beth might be dying of thirst. Familiar ran ahead of him and quickly began to lap the cool water.

"I thought you preferred heavy cream," Omar said as he knelt to stroke the cat. It was strange, but just having Familiar around made him feel closer to Beth. He dipped his hand in the water and rubbed his face. He was bone-tired and worried to the point where he didn't trust his own thinking. He had to find Beth. He couldn't imagine his life without her.

He saw Keya's reflection in the pool before he heard her.

"The people want revenge," she said. "They don't care to hunt for the American woman any longer. They want to go after the men who attacked us."

"Saving Beth and Kaf are the first priorities. In case you've forgotten," Omar said, barely containing his anger, "Kaf is our future."

"The horse is the future you see for us. The horse and the woman. I see a different future. The people have chosen my vision of the future, not yours."

Omar had known that while he was out in the desert searching for Beth, Keya had been busy. It was difficult for him to believe that she'd turned his people against him. Still, she'd had many months when he'd been in Alexandria and traveling from horse farm to horse farm, selecting the right mares to breed to Kaf. In a way, it was almost as if he'd invited her to mutiny.

"I see," he said, scooping up some water and drinking from his hand. He saw the black cat bristling as Keya stepped closer to him. Familiar didn't like her.

"That's all you have to say?" Keya demanded.

Omar stood up. "Good luck. If the people have chosen you to lead them, I have no desire to stand in the way." Even as he said it, he felt as if a tremendous weight had been lifted from his shoulders. "Perhaps

Harad made the right choice. Now I have the freedom to find out.''

''The woman is dead,'' Keya said. ''You might as well accept it.''

''You sound so certain. You must have seen it in a vision.'' Omar couldn't stop himself from goading Keya a little.

''Damn you,'' she whispered, her hands clenching. ''No one in this tribe has had a vision in ten years. Your mother was the last.''

''You're wrong, Keya. I had a vision. In it I saw Beth standing outside my tent. Kaf was behind her, and at her side was my daughter. Our daughter. The rightful heir to the temple of Con.''

''You're making this up,'' Keya accused.

''No, I'm not. I'll find Beth, and we'll return here. Then we'll see which ruler the people prefer. For the moment, though, take the power and see how you fare with it. I have more important things to do than argue with you.''

The horse had drunk its fill and Omar led it away, never once looking over his shoulder at the tall, proud woman who stared after him.

THIS KEYA WOULD BE a handsome woman under different circumstances, like if she'd smile. She has Omar's strong jaw and his intelligent eyes. It's the turn of her mouth that ruins her looks. She's bitter and angry, and I somehow don't think being in power is going to change that.

I think I'll follow her for a while. I'm glad to see there are several other cats in the camp, so I don't stick out like a sore thumb. When I get a chance, I'll have to ask them how they endure traveling around the desert on the back of a horse or camel. There must be a trick to it that I don't know.

Keya is headed for a tent, and she's marching inside as if she owns it, which may indicate that she does. She's a powerhouse. She's going to a chest and opening it. What's she pulling out? It's a map of the desert, and she's studying it. There are some curious marks on it. The oasis where we're currently located is clearly drawn in great detail. Someone has made other marks showing nearby encampments, complete with dates and times. That's what Keya is studying.

There's something else showing, too. A tomb.

I wonder… What is she doing now? She has a walkie-talkie, or some kind of communication device. She's tapping out a code. And someone is answering! My kitty instincts tell me that Keya is the rotten apple that's about to spoil the barrel. Who is she talking to? And what is she saying? As soon as she leaves, I'll snatch the walkie-talkie and take it to Omar. Dang it, she's putting it in her robe. There's nothing left except to take Omar the map. She's leaving it behind.

It's hard for a cat to roll one of these things up, but I'll manage. And I have to hurry. Omar's ready to set out to find Beth, and I think he has to see this before he leaves.

There, I've got it. Now for a mad dash through the settlement. Uh-oh, Keya has seen me and she knows what I've got. She's shrieking like a banshee. Once again the Egyptians' love of cats has saved my hide. I *know she wants to skin me alive, but she can't do it. At least not in front of witnesses.*

Where in the heck is Omar? There he is, and he's finally paying some attention to me.

OMAR UNROLLED THE MAP and looked at it. It was an area he knew by heart. The only thing new were the marks that showed the Cemen encampment and beside them coordinates and specific times and dates. He looked up into Keya's eyes and saw the truth there. ''Why?'' he asked.

''You abandoned us long ago. Your heart has always been torn between the lure of the cities and us. Only a few loyal fools like Yemal hold to their belief in you.'' She glared at the young man who'd come to stand at Omar's side.

''Omar is our true leader,'' Yemal said, glaring at Keya with hatred.

''Not everyone feels as you do, Yemal,'' Keya continued. ''I knew that something had to happen to show everyone that you did not put us first. The people wouldn't follow a man who lost his horses.'' She lifted one shoulder. ''It was simple enough to arrange with Jordel. He has no great love for you or Harad. I've agreed to marry him. He sent the assassin to Alexandria to seal our engagement.''

Omar stared at her. ''So both raids were just a ruse,'' he said almost in a whisper. ''You allowed those men to come in here and injure our people. You let them frighten the women and children, all so that you could make me appear a bad leader. Don't you realize how easily someone could have been killed?''

"No one was seriously hurt."

"Not yet. Beth is out on the desert."

"Bah!" Keya grimaced. "I hope the sand swallows her alive."

Omar nodded to the two men who stood at Keya's side. "Restrain her," he said.

"Me-ow!" Familiar went to Keya and patted up her leg with his paws.

"Get that black devil away from me," Keya snapped, shifting as if she intended to kick the cat.

"Search her," Omar said.

It took the men only seconds to find the walkie-talkie. They handed it to Omar. He held it for a moment. "Who have you been talking to?" he asked.

"None of your damn business." She lifted her chin as if she dared him to do something about it.

"Keya, if anything happens to Beth because of what you've done, I promise that you won't live to see another sunrise."

"Are you suddenly so fond of the desert ways now?" she taunted him. "You won't hurt me, Omar. You'll take me to Alexandria, where the modern courts will mete out some puny punishment. In the city my crimes are nothing."

Omar stepped closer to his cousin. "We are a very long way from the city, Keya. I will not wait for the legal system to judge you if Beth is injured. Now where is she?"

Keya only laughed.

"Who have you been talking to?" Omar held up the walkie-talkie. "Whoever it is must be nearby."

She stopped laughing and looked beyond him.

"You're wasting precious time. While you stand here in the shade, your woman is dying of thirst."

Omar motioned for the guards to take his cousin away. He stood for a moment, watching as she walked tall and proud between the two men.

"What are you going to do?" Mauve asked. She had come up to his side. She took the map from his hand and was looking over it.

"Continue the search."

"Is it possible Beth could have made it to here?" Mauve pointed at the tomb.

"Possible, but unlikely. She didn't even know that it existed."

"Yes, she did," Yemal said. "I told her a little about it."

"Did you tell her who it was intended for?" Omar asked.

Yemal shook his head. "No, I would never have done that."

"Good," Omar said. "Now saddle your horse. We're going after Beth. We'll start with the tomb, and if she isn't there, we'll work our way west. We have to find her. We can't give up hope."

"Meow!" Familiar agreed.

BETH FELT AN OVERPOWERING urge to sleep. She'd been awake most of the night and all morning, and now that she'd had water to drink and shade to cool her, weariness tugged at her body. Kaf and Leah were already dozing as they stood beside her.

The interior of the tomb was cool, and she curled on her side by the water cistern. It was an amazing thing.

Somehow, some way, a well had been dug and the water brought to the surface. In all likelihood the tomb was constructed on a small oasis, but it was still an accomplishment of engineering for the time it was constructed.

A knot of fear was centered in her stomach, but she forced herself to think about the tomb. She'd found a structure that had a direct bearing on her pursuit of Con. She'd studied enough of the symbols that adorned the walls to know that. And when she awoke, she'd study them more closely. Of course, it would be better once she got the lights and cameras and Mauve to help her. For now, though, it was enough to know she was on the right path.

Her eyes drifted closed, and it seemed that only a moment had passed before she heard Kaf snort. The stallion danced beside her, and his snort became a cry of rage.

Disoriented, Beth rolled to a crouch. It was only then that she felt cold steel at her back.

"Don't move, Beth, or you're dead."

John Gilmore's voice was right in her ear.

Chapter Eighteen

Beth hardly dared to breathe as she followed John's directions and rose to her feet. She walked where he directed as he moved slowly around the tomb, studying the intricate carvings and murals that depicted Con as she lay on a couch and dreamed.

"Here is where she foretold the coming of the locust plague." John sounded as if he was carrying on a conversation with a friend. "This is excellent, Beth. You did well to find this."

"It isn't the city—it's only an abandoned tomb," Beth said.

"A little more than that. This is the place where Con came to dream." John tapped her spine gently with the barrel of the gun. "To be honest, my dear, I'm far more interested in this chamber than any lost city."

"What are you talking about?"

"See this?" John pointed to an intricate leaf pattern that was a motif throughout the tomb. It wove in and out of the murals, climbed the columns and decorated the altar, which must have been where Con had lain while she dreamed.

"Yes," Beth said. "It's a design found throughout

all of Con's temples. It was everywhere in the underwater temple.''

"Indeed. I should have known you'd noticed it. You just weren't aware of its importance.''

"Which is?''

John stepped so that he could study her face. "You've always been fair with me, Beth. That should make it harder to kill you, but it won't. But I will satisfy your curiosity before you die. That's my tribute to you as a scientist. You won't die still asking questions.''

"You're generosity is overwhelming.'' Despite her sarcasm, Beth could taste her fear. How many times had she felt that John should be fired? How many gut instincts had she ignored? "Where are the rest of the traitors?''

"Everyone is doing exactly what I told them. Ray is with a band of nomads. I believe they're preparing a raid on Omar Dukhan's settlement. Judy and Sam are helping him. This time, though, it won't be a farce. Omar has been a thorn in our flesh for too long.''

"You can't destroy an entire settlement. There are at least two hundred people there. They haven't done a thing to you.'' Beth started toward John, but stopped when he lifted the gun barrel to her cheekbone.

"Always so noble. Worried about the poor nomads. Did you forget that you won't be around to worry? Now do you want to hear about this leaf or not?''

Beth nodded.

"You see, I bought into your legend of Con long before you thought I did. It fascinated me, a woman with the power to foretell the future. A woman descended from a line of visionaries. I'd heard of such things in desert Indian tribes in the American Southwest and Central America. I also knew there were certain secret rituals that were employed prior to dreaming. All of them in the cases I studied involved some type of hallucinogen. I began to wonder if the same might be true for the visionaries of Egypt. And then I began to notice this curious leaf in all of Con's decor. When we found the underwater temple and I got a clear view of the leaf there, I knew I was on the right track.''

"So what?" Beth asked.

"Patience," John said calmly. "I'm getting to the good part. All the Native American rituals used peyote in some form or other. Yes, they had visions, but not necessarily visions of the future. This was where Con's people were different. So it stood to reason if these women were using some plant as an inducement to visions, that plant worked exclusively on a part of the brain that no other plant did.''

Beth saw it now, a billion-dollar pharmaceutical discovery. It had nothing to do with archaeology or the incredible accomplishments of a woman in the past. It was all about money.

A cold dread swept over her. Her thinking was way too small. Yes, the potential for selling the drug legally was almost unlimited. Illegally, the uses of it could put the power of the world into the hands of a few.

John's chuckle brought her out of her dark thoughts. "So, you begin to see the future. Ah, Beth, you've spent your entire life devoted to the past. In doing so, you've let your future escape you."

"John, you can't do this," Beth said. "In the wrong hands, that drug could—"

"I know exactly what it could do. And I intend to make my buyers pay for it at a premium price."

Beth started to argue but knew it would do no good. "What if there *is* no plant?" she asked. She touched a column with the climbing vine carved into it. "What if this is simply a design that Con preferred, like my love of wisteria?"

"Then my backer has gambled a fortune for nothing. Although I am mourning the loss of my comrades in an unexplained desert attack, I will continue on to search for the lost city." He grinned at his cleverness.

"And Mauve?"

"She's conveniently ridden out to Omar's people. She will die there. You see, Beth, the thing about pulling off an illegal act is to make sure there aren't any loose ends."

"Judy?"

John shrugged. "She's so desperate for fame that she won't question anything we tell her. She might suspect something underhanded, but I don't think it will trouble her conscience for long. If it's any consolation, Judy, Ray and Sam only joined my plan once they realized the potential for making money."

Beth's last hope was Omar—if he hadn't been killed in the desert the night before.

"Since you've told me everything else, who's your backer?" Beth asked.

"A very wealthy and powerful man. One you know but have never met." He grinned. "Nazar Bettina."

Beth gasped. "Why?"

"He's a man who likes to bet on both horses in a race," John explained, "but he always knows his favorite, and that horse always wins. Mr. Bettina knew you could find the way to the lost city. You were the better scientist when it came to actually finding the location." John walked over and untied the valise from Kaf's saddle. The stallion danced nervously but didn't attempt to run away. "He also knew you would keep him informed of your every move. His judgment of your character was that you wouldn't go along with letting him have the plant, once we determined exactly what it was. So I was sent along to finish what you started."

"We haven't found the lost city," Beth said, stalling for time.

"True, but I don't think I'm going to need it." His gaze drifted around the empty tomb. "This is where the answer will be found. This is the dream chamber." His fingertips caressed one of the vine carvings that wound around the neck of a feline. "The answer is here. Can't you feel it, Beth?"

She could. As the afternoon light slanted into the dream chamber, she saw that the walls were almost alive with depictions of the plant. She'd never seen a vine that even resembled the five-leaf plant, which incorporated an irislike flower. But if it was possible to identify the plant and find it, John Gilmore would. He was a detail man and thorough at whatever job he took on. Somehow he had to be stopped. As did Nazar Bettina.

John walked to the opening of the tomb and listened for a moment. "I thought I heard something."

"Expecting company?" Beth asked.

"Yes, I am. Ray and some of the Bedouins on his payroll should be arriving soon. We took the equipment from the hotel, Beth. You won't be needing it. But I should take care of you before the others get here. Those three are greedy, but they have a squeamish streak. They might also get the idea that if I'd kill you, I might kill them." He laughed. "Wouldn't that be a shame if they had to worry about such a thing?"

There was a movement at the entrance of the dream chamber, and Beth almost started. A small, black shadow disengaged itself from the entrance and darted toward the altar.

Familiar! She recognized the cat and felt a tide of hope.

"What?" John must have seen her expression change. He turned around and saw only the empty entrance. "What?" he demanded.

"I saw a woman standing there," Beth said. "She was wearing a pale-yellow robe, and her dark hair was braided over one shoulder." Beth was describing the underwater statue of Con that she knew John had seen.

"Stop it." He inched backward so that he had both the entrance and Beth in sight.

"There!" Beth pointed to a dark corner of the room. "There she is!"

John whirled, swinging the gun in a wide arc. "There's nothing there!" he said angrily. "What are you trying to do?"

"She's in here," Beth whispered. "Remember the legend, John. Only those of her blood knew her secrets." Beth leaned toward him and whispered, "Anyone else who tried always died a strange and gruesome death.''

''Like the mummy's curse,'' John said sarcastically. He'd been rattled but now seemed recovered. ''A nice try, Beth, but you can't scare me off this.''

A rock clattered against the far wall of the temple. For all of his brave words, John whirled and fired, the shot echoing in the chamber.

''What was that?'' Beth asked in her most terrified voice. ''Who's in here with us? What if there really *is* a curse?''

''Stop it.'' John's voice was harsh.

Another rock pinged the wall, and a long, low growl emanated from behind the altar. It was eerie enough that even though Beth knew it was Familiar, the hair on the back of her neck stood on end.

John swung back around to face the altar. He pushed Beth roughly to the ground and walked toward the nerve-jangling sound.

Familiar sprang out from behind the altar, a black shadow that flew through the air with the unearthly yowl of a spirit in hell.

Caught off guard, John fired wildly, missing the cat. He stepped backward, and Beth moved her leg so that he tripped over it. As he fell, the gun went flying.

Beth saw the weapon land and she scrambled for it just as John went after it, too. For one split second, both of their hands closed on the weapon. Beth held the barrel and John the grip. Though she tried to hold it away from her, the barrel was moved slowly to her chest.

''Let it go,'' John said coldly.

There was a distinct click, and Beth looked up into Omar's blazing eyes. He held a revolver at John's ear. "Put the gun down," he said coldly.

"I can kill her before you stop me," John threatened, unwilling to obey.

"Perhaps you can. But then I promise that you will die a million deaths in pain and torment that you've never dreamed of. If Beth is harmed, no amount of searching the desert will ever reveal your fate, but you have my word that you will suffer endlessly."

Very slowly John lowered the gun.

"Ray and the others are with the people who attacked your village!" Beth said, the words tumbling out of her mouth. "They're going back to kill everyone!"

"I don't think that will happen," Omar replied as he knelt beside Beth and scooped her against his chest. "Harad located the Cemen tribe with helicopters. Jordel and the Americans have been taken into custody. They're on their way to an Alexandria jail as we speak."

Beth clung to Omar, unable, now that it was over, to control her trembling. "I was so afraid," she whispered.

"You're safe," Omar said. His lips brushed the top of her head. "And Kaf is safe because of you." He stood, pulling her up with him. "You saved the future of my people."

"Beth!" Mauve rushed into the chamber, stopping after only a few feet and looking around in awe. "Man, what *is* this place?"

"It's incredible, isn't it," Beth said, some life returning to her voice. "This is where Con came—" She felt Omar's arm tighten around her in silent warning. He didn't want her to talk about the place.

"It's actually a tomb," Omar said carefully. "Con was to be buried here, but she wasn't. After Herakleion fell, she abandoned this site and returned to Cairo."

Mauve looked from Beth to Omar, a question on her face but one she did not voice.

"How do you know that?" Beth asked. She picked up the black cat and snuggled him close. He was one brave kitty. Omar stroked Familiar's head as he considered his answer.

"It's a long story," he finally said. "One I should have told you when we first met. But tonight, I'll tell you the whole thing. Let us first deliver John to my brother. The helicopters should be here any moment. Then we'll take Kaf back to the oasis, and I'll tell you the truth."

OMAR BROUGHT the tray of wine. The last rosy rays of the sun cast half his face in shadow as he served Beth and then took a goblet and settled down beside her. Instead of the settlement, he'd chosen a secluded place beside the pool at the oasis. Kaf and Leah stood only a few paces away, and Familiar, sated with goat cheese and milk, lay sleeping at Beth's side.

"Why do I get the feeling that I'm not going to like the truth?" Beth asked. She'd been dreading this moment since Omar had revealed an unexpected knowledge of Con's last days. She'd spent the remainder of the afternoon putting together a lot of clues. The picture she came up with was of a guide who knew a lot more than he'd ever let on.

But until Omar spoke, she could cling to the illusion that he'd been her hero, the man who rescued her. That was what she wanted to believe.

"The lost City of Con is a four-day ride from here," Omar said. "I'll take you there tomorrow."

"You know where it is?" Beth had been prepared for a confession, but not one of this magnitude.

"I know it well."

"How?"

"I am the defender of the lost city. My bloodline descends directly from Con. I am her heir, and these are her people. Our job is to protect the lost city and the secrets of Con from all outsiders."

The words, so simply spoken, were like splinters of steel in Beth's heart.

"You knew I was looking for the city, and so you hired on as a guide with the intent of deliberately misleading me." Beth put the glass of wine down in the sand. It had grown bitter on her tongue.

"I had no choice. My vow to my people was sacred."

Beth felt the splinters slide deeper into her heart. "And you figured the easiest way to manipulate me was to lure me into bed. Not only would you destroy my reputation and make me a laughingstock, you would make me feel cheap and debased. How clever." She rose to her feet. "I'll find the lost city, Omar. Without your help."

He grasped her hand. "I'll take you there in the morning."

"And break your vow? I wouldn't ask that of you." She could see that her words stung him, and she wanted to hurt him more.

"I believe that once you understand what's at stake, you might forgive me, Beth."

"A man of honor would never have hired on as my guide. You were willing to sacrifice me to save—"

"My heritage," he interrupted. "You would do the same for the Corbets. I know you would."

"I would protect my family, that's true. But I don't think I would do it the way you have. I honestly don't. I don't have it in me to use someone the way you used me."

Omar didn't flinch under her attack. "I cursed myself for a fool the morning after I made love with you," he said softly. "I knew that I had crossed a line. But I couldn't stop myself, Beth. I couldn't deny myself that one chance to know you in the most intimate way a man can know a woman."

"So you gratified your needs," Beth lashed out. "I'm glad I was available." She had never felt such pain. She would have struck him if she thought it would help.

He reached up and gently touched her face. "You're so far from the truth. I knew then that I loved you. I knew that my vow and your pursuit of the village would forever separate us. So I took the one chance I had. Once I realized that I had fallen in love with you, I couldn't pretend I didn't want you. You wanted me, too, Beth. We'd made each other no promises on that night. We simply took what we both wanted."

"That's very modern of you, Omar. What about all

the bull about holding out for the one woman who was your fate? Was that just another pretty line?''

"No, Beth. It's the truth. You're the woman I love. Even if you leave here hating me, I'll continue to love you until I die."

"I must say, you have a persuasive way with words. I've already been immunized against you, though." To Beth's horror, she found that her anger, along with the pain and humiliation, were lessening.

Omar caught her hand and brought it to his chest. "Listen to this, Beth. To my heart." He put his hand on her chest. "Listen with *your* heart. I am not perfect. I was wrong in some things. But I love you. I'm here now, willing to show you the very thing that I've vowed to protect."

Beth's heart was racing. The pain had changed, from one of betrayal to something else. Omar's words were touching her. And she was afraid to allow it.

"John's theory about the plants I told you about," she said. "Was it accurate?"

Omar held on to her hand. "Sit with me. Let me talk."

The pain in Beth's chest was a throb, but she sank back onto the pillows. In a way, she did understand what Omar had done. But understanding didn't take away the reality of his betrayal.

"John was correct about the plants. Con, her predecessors and descendants, used a plant they called the orbus. It gave certain users the ability to dream the future."

"Certain users?"

"Descendants of Con." He paused. "Some believe

that my mother's people were not from Egypt, but from the sky.'' He waited for her reaction.

"Aliens?"

"That is one theory. Another is that something in our DNA allowed us to use the plant in a way that others could not.''

"And do you have that ability?'' Beth asked. She wasn't certain what she was feeling. The things Omar was telling her sounded like something in a science-fiction novel.

"I don't know. I never had the chance. Long ago the cultivation of the plant was stopped. My mother, Aleta, used the last of the plant when I was a small child. It is extinct.''

Beth examined his face in the fading light of the sun. Dusk had begun to steal over them, and on the eastern horizon the first stars were out.

"Is this another fabrication? Another lie designed to protect your people? Because if it is, don't bother. That plant could be the most destructive weapon known to humankind. Even if I knew that it existed, I wouldn't tell.''

Omar's hand glided through the soft night to touch her cheek. "I know that, Beth. That's why I'm telling you all this. Whatever the price, I know I must trust you. With my past and my future. I realize that you can't share my future if I withhold my past from you.''

"I have no future in Egypt, Omar. My expedition is in shambles. According to your brother and his sources, there's no such person as Nazar Bettina. There's no trace of the man who backed me.'' Beth paused for breath. "The only thing I can do is return to my job in Arizona."

"You could stay here."

"In Alexandria?"

"Here. In the desert. With me."

"What are you saying?" Beth felt a new ripple of emotion. The hard crust of anger was cracking around her heart.

"Marry me, Beth. Live in the desert with me. I've watched you. I don't think it would be a hardship for you to leave the luxuries of the modern world behind. I'll show you the lost city, and I'll teach you all the secrets of Con. You'll bear her daughters." He cupped her chin and tilted it up as he moved his lips closer. "And sons."

Beth could hardly think straight. "What if I decide to reveal your secrets to the world?"

Omar kissed her lips lightly. "I can only explain to you my role among my people. I realize that the modern world will eventually catch up with us. I can't stop it forever. If your heart determines that you must be the one to reveal the lost city, then you will do that. I believe in you, Beth. I believe you'll make the right decision. For yourself, for me and for my people."

The last bit of anger fell away. Beth knew that Omar had been torn. But in protecting his people, he had also protected her. And in loving her, he'd learned to trust not only her, but himself.

"We'll start for the lost city tomorrow," Omar said. "It will amaze you. It's the custom of my people that the ruler is married in the temple there. It will take some arranging, but we can manage the ceremony within the week."

"Is there a reason for the rush?" Beth asked. "I'd like for my family to have time to come."

"The journey to Con's city is long and difficult. We'll have another ceremony for your family in Alexandria," Omar said. "We must marry by the end of the week."

"Why?" Beth asked again.

"It is the moon of Con in July. We must have the ceremony on the full moon, in her temple, at midnight, so that our marriage will be blessed in every way."

Beth kissed his lips. "You're superstitious!"

He pulled her into his arms. "I live in a country that worships cats and ancient gods. Of course I'm superstitious. Do you object to a hasty wedding? Are you having second thoughts?"

Beth shook her head. Marriage to Omar was a far bigger adventure than she'd bargained for when she left America. Her life would be traveling with nomads, raising magnificent horses that flew over the desert sands—and sharing her bed and her life with the man she loved. "No second thoughts," she whispered.

Omar stood and pulled her to her feet. "Then come with me to my tent. I think we should practice being married."

"I'd like that," Beth said, falling into step beside him as they walked toward Omar's tent.

I'LL HEAD BACK to Alexandria tomorrow. Mauve, I understand, is staying to do some work in Con's dream chamber. From the rumors I hear, Mica is staying to help her. Just to be on the safe side.

Harad has returned to the city, along with his cousin, Keya. Omar and Harad rounded up all those responsible for the attacks on the settlement, and they had an appointment with the Alexandria police. I could see that it was tough for the brothers to opt for town justice for their cousin. I wonder if Omar and Harad will actually allow Keya to stand trial. I've heard some rumors that they intend to banish her from the tribe forever. I think a jail term would be more appropriate, but banishment would hurt her the most. Sometimes desert justice is more effective than the legal system.

The only fly in the ointment is that no trace has been found of Nazar Bettina. The phone number Beth had for the man was an empty office in Alexandria. Harad is still pursuing all leads to track down the moneybags behind all of this.

And that Harad, what a brother! When he realized Omar was in love with Beth, he started checking her out. When he discovered that she was an orphan, he began to realize that Beth might be the perfect woman to fit into Omar's life. Though she loves the Corbets and they love her, she can start a new life in the desert. And Beth won't miss the conveniences of a more civilized life.

Speaking of civilized, I have to get back to Alexandria. Peter and Eleanor will be frantic. And then there's the little issue of Amelia. She's winging her way to Egypt right this moment. And I'm ready for a little civilization.

Yes, it'll be nice to stroll the streets, hunting down

the best seafood and listening to the commentary of the city cats. This was a terrific adventure, but I'm due for some R&R.

I can't wait to get home and tell Clotilde all about this. She's going to think I'm a regular superhero. I think just to refresh my memory, I'll take another stroll around the camp. Horses, camels, the black night settling over the desert. How many American kitties have seen this sight?

You know, it's wonderful being me.

HARLEQUIN®
INTRIGUE®

**What do a sexy Texas cowboy, a brooding
Chicago lawyer and a mysterious
Arabian sheikh have in common?**

By day, these agents pursue lives of city professionals; by
night they are specialized government operatives. Men
bound by love, loyalty and the law—they've vowed to
keep their missions and identities confidential....

You loved the Texas and Montana series. Now head to
Chicago where the assignments are top secret, the city
nights, dangerous and the passion is just heating up!

NOT ON HIS WATCH
by CASSIE MILES
July 2002

LAYING DOWN THE LAW
by ANN VOSS PETERSON
August 2002

PRINCE UNDER COVER
by ADRIANNE LEE
September 2002

Available at your favorite retail outlet.

HARLEQUIN®
Makes any time special®

Who was she really?

Where Memories Lie

GAYLE WILSON

AMANDA STEVENS

Two full-length novels of enticing, romantic suspense—by two favorite authors.

They don't remember their names or lives, but the two heroines in these two fascinating novels do know one thing: they are women of passion. Can love help bring back the memories they've lost?

Look for WHERE MEMORIES LIE in July 2002—
wherever books are sold.

Princes...Princesses...
London Castles...New York Mansions...
To live the life of a royal!

**In 2002, Harlequin Books lets you escape to a
world of royalty with these royally themed titles:**

Temptation:
January 2002—*A Prince of a Guy* (#861)
February 2002—*A Noble Pursuit* (#865)

American Romance:
The Carradignes: American Royalty (Editorially linked series)
March 2002—*The Improperly Pregnant Princess* (#913)
April 2002—*The Unlawfully Wedded Princess* (#917)
May 2002—*The Simply Scandalous Princess* (#921)
November 2002—*The Inconveniently Engaged Prince* (#945)

Intrigue:
The Carradignes: A Royal Mystery (Editorially linked series)
June 2002—*The Duke's Covert Mission* (#666)

Chicago Confidential
September 2002—*Prince Under Cover* (#678)

The Crown Affair
October 2002—*Royal Target* (#682)
November 2002—*Royal Ransom* (#686)
December 2002—*Royal Pursuit* (#690)

Harlequin Romance:
June 2002—*His Majesty's Marriage* (#3703)
July 2002—*The Prince's Proposal* (#3709)

Harlequin Presents:
August 2002—*Society Weddings* (#2268)
September 2002—*The Prince's Pleasure* (#2274)

Duets:
September 2002—*Once Upon a Tiara/Henry Ever After* (#83)
October 2002—*Natalia's Story/Andrea's Story* (#85)

**Celebrate a year of royalty with
Harlequin Books!**

Available at your favorite retail outlet.

HARLEQUIN®
Makes any time special ®

Visit us at www.eHarlequin.com

HSROY02

Three masters of the romantic suspense
genre come together in this special
Collector's Edition!

Unveiled

NEW YORK TIMES BESTSELLING AUTHORS

TESS GERRITSEN
STELLA CAMERON

And Harlequin Intrigue® author

AMANDA STEVENS

Nail-biting mystery…heart-pounding sensuality…and
the temptation of the unknown come together in one
magnificent trade-size volume. These three talented
authors bring stories that will give you thrills *and*
chills like never before!

Coming to your favorite retail outlet in August 2002.

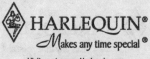

HARLEQUIN®
Makes any time special®

Visit us at www.eHarlequin.com

PHU